For Barry Donohoo.

THE PAST TRADER

A.M. Donohoo

The Past Trader

1.

She kissed her love as the sun set but tasted only tobacco. They were standing together on the bustling concrete boardwalk that hemmed the city from the beach. Flip-flopped foot traffic flowed around them as if they didn't exist - as if they were young lovers stuck upon their own island of time. Through one distracted eye she caught the sun's final flash - a red line that smeared blood from the sky. She broke from the kiss.

Marco was a cheap date. She had seen the stress at the edges of his eyes when the bill had arrived. Had felt affection for his feigned indifference and total insistence on picking up the check. Money: so precious to him when to her it meant nothing. The dinner had cost orders of magnitude less than her portfolio's price movement on any given day. About five millionths of one percent of her book she calculated in the back of her mind.

"What are you thinking about my love?" He asked.

"Nothing." She said, hugging closer. "Thank you for dinner."

She knew she needed to break up with him. Had known it for a while. But she was dragging the present with her as far into the future as she could.

"Will you miss this city?" Marco asked.

"I'll be back soon enough."

Bicycles pedaled through the sepia glow along the winding concrete path between the boardwalk and the sea. Palm trees carved stark silhouettes. She watched the bicycle vectors through space, imagining their wake in time. Wavefronts of coincidence and creation emerging at all points behind them and ahead, but collapsed only to now, only to this. The entirety of the past and the future mere illusion.

"But you can't wait for me." She insisted.

"What if I came with you?"

"Your time is here Marco. Mine is elsewhere."

He thought about this. It was one of the things she liked most about him. He always thought before he reacted. In another life his mind could have been honed to greatness.

He nodded slowly.

He was a musician - an artist - and a good looking man in LA - what they had together was real, but he was on a rising tide, and she knew that his burning affection for her would soon smolder beneath relentless waves of lovers and liaisons. He wasn't going to shed a tear. It wasn't his style. She would never have dated him if it was.

He kissed her on the forehead - a baptism: "Enigma is your name."

"Enigma Dandieu, can you imagine?"

"It would be a good step in your career as a super villain." He said, teasing. Mostly.

"You would have made an incredible henchman."

"I'll always be your henchman." He looked her in the eye and paused for a few beats… *those blue eyes*… "Unless, like I'm dating someone else or something." He added unnecessarily.

She punched his chest. "Just burp on my dreams."

"Hey, you're the one bringing things to a terminus."

"Ugh. I know." She broke from the hug and straightened her jacket, a silk mini tuxedo coat with velvet lapels like daggers. The California air freshened as she stepped away from his nicotine musk. A sea breeze off the Pacific. She took his hand to lead him away from the beach-side restaurant down the boardwalk towards Santa Monica.

"How long's the flight to Tokyo?" He asked.

She considered the question, feeling the gears in her mind start to shift, the patterns overlapping, the edge coming to the fore - the conversations she needed to have with Shintaro. The terms of the deal she needed to offer Tatsuma. The changes in cash flow. "It should be about 14 hours door-to-door." She answered after a moment. "If I'm lucky."

"I'm surprised your company doesn't fly you. You're a hot-shot. Surely they have a private jet."

A wry smile crossed her lips, *the thought of The House having a jet.*

"We're not that kind of company..."

"But surely you can afford it."

"Ha. That's most certainly not the point."

"How much would it cost? Do you know?"

"What?"

"To fly private to Japan?"

"Hmm... probably about one fifty. More if you were in a hurry."

"One hundred and fifty thousand dollars?!"

"Give or take. Depends on whether you own the jet."

"Fuck."

About seven thousandth of one percent of her portfolio she calculated.

"Wow... that's more than I've made in my entire lifetime probably."

She turned back to him and pulled him down by the neck to kiss him on the forehead - a baptism: "Money isn't everything."

"Have you ever flown private before?" He asked.

She shrugged. "It's come up. A few times. For short haul flights. They're kind of underwhelming. Like airborne limousines with incredibly awkward bathrooms."

He nodded, not believing her. "Do you at least fly business class?"

"Of course. We're thrifty darling, we're not psychotic."

*   *   *

She was approaching her thirteenth year as an employee of The House. The House was founded in 1929 on the eve of the Great Depression. For a while it had been ironically referred to as the Timing Fund for this inauspicious moment of inception, but decades later the name cut too close to the bone, and was discarded for its lack of opacity. You may have heard of The House if you pay close attention to the news, or work in finance. Publicly, The House's core enterprise is known by a different name, but to insiders it's only ever called The House. In the popular imagination it's one of those staid, dry, back-of-the-room, middlemen sorts of companies, that nobody quite understands, and that fewer still are interested in. But through a gordian knot of subsidiaries, shells, associates, members, partners, investments, investors, and holdings, The House is one of the ten most powerful organizations on earth. The others mostly being companies that we own major stakes in, or governments that those companies more or less control.

The Past Trader

Of course power is heavily overstated. The tides
of humanity are governed by coincidence, chaos, and hive
optimization. We find reassurance in the idea of captains and
levers, and of people holding more control over the world than
ourselves, but the truth is infinitely complex, and power scales
surprisingly weakly.

But The House does have power. For what it's worth.

The House always wins.

*   *   *

Marco waved goodbye to her with a final, stoic, bewildered sort of
a look. From the back seat of her limousine she watched him for a
few blinks as he faded to a darkened mass beneath a sulfur street-
light. Then she took her laptop from her bag to answer emails.

The first was from Shintaro.

> *Miss Tallulah,*
> *We're going to need to short the ancestors of Dow Chemical*
> *and Standard Oil. At least $100 mil a piece. $200 mil*
> *would be better. We must eviscerate Dow.*
>
> *Currencies will have to be calibrated for blood loss. We still*
> *need to do a lot more work on that. VWX moves should be*
> *predictable but we should optimise beyond them. For longs*
> *we must include Pantikapaion Chemical and a small outfit*
> *called Banthour. Their line is crystal clear to me.*

See you in a few days. <u>Don't</u> trust Tatsuma, he's the worst cannibal in The House.
S.

She thought about her reply for a minute, watching West LA's beige world of strip malls and stucco pass her by in a sooty blur.

Shintaro san,
Thank you for the additional thoughts. Thrilled you're on this deal. Will look further into Pan Chem. Banthour is high on the radar.

Tatsuma's reputation precedes him. Fear not - I will keep a tight grip on my cutlery. I also make for a poor tooth pick.

See you on the near side,
Tallie

2.

She arrived at the check-in counter at LAX and upgraded herself to first class. She wanted a proper sleep before arriving in Tokyo, and Marco's quizzing about private jets had made her feel like a cheapskate. *You only live once. Probably.* She put the seat upgrade on to her personal account. She was likely senior enough in The House that nobody would question her expenses, but a first class flight was perceived as awfully gauche and somewhat dangerous.

She was briskly escorted through security to the first class lounge, where she opened her computer to work during the thirty minutes she had before departure. The trade she was planning to make required almost nine billion dollars atop the entirety of her existing capital. It would be her largest trade to date. The problem was that she wasn't sure that an extra nine billion would be enough.

Marius, her mentor, had always hammered into her that bigger was better: "*Take what you think the right price is, and add ten percent to it. Otherwise you'll underbid.*" She was stewing on this. Borrowing $9.9 billion - let's just round to ten - was a lot for a trader of her seniority. But the upside…

A man entering the lounge caught her attention.

He wore a leather jacket and a shrunken black tee that betrayed a cantilevered gut exceeding slightly-too-tight jeans.

Seeing her, his head tilted in recognition and he made a beeline towards her.

"Are you going to miss this city?" He asked Tallulah, collapsing into the chair opposite.

"No. Have we met?"

"Meeting is such a quaint concept. What's the difference between knowing someone for a moment or knowing them for a lifetime?"

"There's a lot more choice involved in knowing someone for a lifetime."

"Ahh, but then you don't have any choice with knowing *family*… You don't have any family." The sentence was almost posed as a question, but was enough like a statement that her guard went up to her battlements.

"Excuse me?"

"Sorry, wrong foot. I'm Fred. You can call me Fred. I'm looking to make a trade, and I was told to keep an eye out for you."

Tallie tasted venom. "A trade? Why do you presume I'm in the market for what you're trading?"

A cheshire cat grin: "Tallie, Tallie, I'm so sorry, I've made such a hash of this. My mother always used to tell me, *think before you speak*. I'm still working on that. So here's the thinking that came first: I have some Antecedent Options from the '70s. Reach back to '65. Heard you might be interested. Heard you were making a play."

"Antecedents? What volume."

"$26 million. Local frame."

Tallie's eyebrows lifted. The man took this as an approval to signal the waitress for a drink: "A beer. European. No IPAs or Californian shit."

"Stella Artois?" The waitress suggested.

"Fine."

The Past Trader

The man sat back and scratched his chest, his eyes not wavering from hers. "So, are you interested?"

Tallie crossed her arms skeptically. "Look... Fred. I don't do business in airline lounges with strangers without provenance. Most especially when they know who I am but haven't had the manners to make an appointment through a regular channel. So..." she inspected her nails. "Who the fuck are you, how do you know about what I do, and what makes you think I'd be interested in trading *with you*?"

His same Cheshire smile was joined by hands up in surrender. "I am genuinely sorry to have made such a bad impression. But I understand - to some extent - how a deal like this works, and I don't trust any of the vipers that work out of your shop. So I thought... discretion, you know?

"I'm an entrepreneur by trade," he continued, leaning back in his chair in a self-satisfied way "developed a bunch of ad technology back in the day, high speed digital marketing stuff. I sold my company and made a bit... A friend of mine, he knew about your industry and saw this... *distressed opportunity* let's call it, someone needing to sell a lot in a hurry, and this friend of mine, he knew I was looking at where to park some cash. This friend he says to me: 'How would you like to own history?'

"I mean what a pitch. Are you kidding? Own history? I lapped it up. I'm an engineer you see, by training. Had some understanding of physics and whatnot. Enough to get myself in trouble. So this alternate perception of time really caught my imagination. History as residual matter annihilation? *Tradable pasts?* Shit was catnip to me.

"So…" he sighed, "like a fucking idiot I bought 100 million dollars worth of magic beans. Paid in cash. Then, right after the trade - maybe unrelated - this friend of mine goes AWOL, like totally off the map. Never heard from him again. And so I spend the next few years completely ashamed of myself, thinking I had parked my once-in-a-lifetime windfall into buying the Brooklyn Bridge, you know what I mean?"

Tallie nodded once, curtly.

"But then I start getting calls. Strangers. In real nice suits. Weird stuff. People in blacked out cars, appearing then vanishing. Offering me *serious money* for these *antecedent options*. I start to realize that these things might not be magic beans after all."

The waitress placed the beer and a coaster on the low table in front of the man. He snatched it immediately and took a long gulp. "You sure you don't want to join me?"

She shook her head.

He shrugged and drank more, "So I started to get a bit smarter about what I actually owned. Tried to understand how it could affect things. Like how the past might impact the future. Or the present impact the… past or… whatever. Met some people in your industry. Used some of those mysterious contacts I had made. I'm not a boat shaker -" his hands went up in surrender again, "- just a capitalist. But that's kind of what brought me to this juncture. To this exact present. If you follow me."

"And how the fuck did you find me at LAX?"

"Ahh, well. That part wasn't so hard. I'm a bit annoyed you decided to fly first class though. I thought that wasn't the style of you guys." He looked around the room and the elegant settings - low tables and comfortable chairs in muted colors, gentle lighting - "that tells me something about you I think. Or is that a false signal?"

"You didn't answer my question."

"No, I guess I didn't. Anyway…" He necked half of the remaining beer then burped softly and wiped his mouth. "I decided to come to you in person rather than through an agent so you could take something of a measure of me. Not sure if that was a mistake or not… I mean I didn't want to interrupt your nice dinner you had earlier with your boyfriend. But here's my card." he tried to hand her a card. She remained passive, so he placed it in front of her. It was a blank piece of cardboard with an encrypted email address written on it in ballpoint pen: *Fred-v89261x@protonmail.com*. Tallie felt her blood boil.

"Drop me a line some time and I'll send you my proofs and particulars. I do really want to make this deal," the man said breezily. "I already have a good sense of the assets I'd like to sell. And I'd like to do a few pasts swaps - this won't be a pure cash transaction - and I'm led to believe that you could facilitate that. So, anyway… it's been a pleasure meeting you Tallie. I really am sorry for the rudeness and the subterfuge. It isn't my style, but then this isn't a normal business."

He offered a handshake then thought better of it and looked towards the door. As he twisted his head she saw beads of sweat on the edges of his brow. He smiled furtively and was revealed to her. The lens inverted and the picture zoomed away and up, leaving him as a balding worm at her feet.

"You're trying to change your fortune." She said to him slowly - calmly but with menace. "Change your past."

He paused mid standing. "Just… just small tweaks."

"You've spoken to a lineweaver."

He returned carefully to his seat. "Yes. That's who gave me your name. You were recommended, amongst others."

Tallie tilted her head on its side and gave him her most reptilian stare. The man was desperate.

"...I know that this sort of commission doesn't come cheap or - or..." He began to get flustered. "But when I heard what you were working on I knew that I *fortuitously* had something that you could trade so -"

"How did you know what I was working on?"

"I... paid for some information."

"To your lineweaver?"

"No. I can't say. I just knew that the pasts I own are extremely valuable, that you can use them. Trade them. But I was told that I had to find someone who was working a play in the right reference frame."

"Hmm." She calmed herself and carefully stretched her arms, conveying maximum disinterest. "I don't normally do over the counter trades. It's not really how I make money."

His eyes followed across her arms, then down her breasts, all the way to her legs. *He's straight*, she noted.

"What's so bad about your life now that you want to change?" She asked.

His eyes snapped back to hers. "Did you grow up in poverty?"

She didn't answer.

"I did." He nodded, "Not real poverty, like in Africa or Bangladesh or... whatever, but there were chances that I missed. Opportunities that I should have been given."

"But you say that you're successful now. You don't think that's attributable to those hardships?"

"Maybe it is. But I could be more successful."

"Yes, and you could be less successful too."

"I think I have enough capital to weight that in my favor -"

"That's to be seen." She took a long breath and paused for a few heartbeats. "And frankly not my concern. I'm open to considering making this trade for you."

"Great, that's..."

"But I'll need your lineweaver's full analysis. And none of this James Bond shit. And if you ever, ever attempt to intimidate me again, or have me fucking followed, there will be *consequences.*"

"I understand. That wasn't my..."

"Now fuck off, take *my* card -" she reached into her bag "- only contact me by email, and have a nice fucking day."

He took her card and stared at it in his hands. Like she had handed him his death warrant. Perhaps she had she realized - not caring. *Did she care?* No, she decided.

"Yeah. Ok." He put her card in his wallet and threw a $20 note on the table. "Enjoy Japan."

The Past Trader

3.

The House has a blended portfolio of assets and strategies. Everything from equities, to bonds, real estate trusts, commodities, FX, derivatives, and futures. But I work in our most important team which delivers our highest profits.

I trade *pasts*.

Whenever we share an experience with our friends, it's common that each person's recollection of the event differs afterwards - sometimes slightly, sometimes wildly.

The popular assumption is that it's the mind that's to blame for the divergence - that the past exists as a clear and inalienable road that we have traveled along together. Across a perfect chain of causation.

So we presume that it's our flawed memories that stumble over the detail of that inviolable path.

But *in fact* the past is just as in flux as the future. The present is woven from infinite disparate lines, and these lines wrap and warp in a constant re-weaving. The fabric of the present is all that exists - everything else is just a frame-dragging effect that our brains have evolved to process and store as a fiction that we call history.

Of course memories **are** imperfect - they are a completely unreliable electrochemical simulation. But the popular mistake is assuming that the coincidence is the feature.

A lifeform - or for that matter a table or a book - is a sustained concentration of nuclear energy. That concentration forges a line - a density in space time that slices a unique pinhole through a tangled universe of seething chaos. Ultimately entropy dissipates all such concentrations, and we die, or burn, or dissolve, and dematerialize back into the quantum vacuum.

But money and capital have a sort of a *gravity* to them within the chaos - a tiny, almost imperceptible weight - but there. The gravity of capital can change things both in the future and in the past. Nobody's entirely sure of why this is. My own thesis is that because capital has such an impact on the future and on the shape of things to come, it bends both directions by symmetry.

A good pasts trader doesn't make investments to improve the cash yields from the future, they enhance the profitability of the present. The right capital deployed in the right place will subtly alter history and improve today's earnings and valuations. The records themselves shift - history changes - the flawed memory of what *was* becomes stupefied under the archaeological plasticity of what *is*.

Of course this makes measuring the actual profits from pasts trading difficult. Much of our labor has been spent perfecting the tools and techniques we use to measure our profit from changes to history. This is The House's edge.

And today, skipped forward within the ceaseless present, The House controls almost two trillion in assets. We could of course control more, but finding good help is difficult.

*   *   *

Somewhat to my surprise, Yuko was waiting for me at arrivals. My temporary move to Tokyo had taken a lot of finessing from The House, and Yuko had spearheaded the diplomacy that had brought me in as a foreign resident with no quarantine schedule more than a week before the public restrictions were due to lift.

Yuko was dressed sharply in dark sunglasses, a pin-striped pencil skirt, matching jacket with an avant garde cut, and kitten heels. She lifted one hand to wave. Her suited driver bowed and took my luggage. He wore a mask, rubber gloves, and a face shield.

"Hello Bonsai Anarchist." I greeted Yuko. "This is unexpected."

A laconic smile. "How the hell are you Tallie?"

Yuko's accent was pure London, with a hint of cockney drawl - an impressive achievement, given she had barely spoken a word of English until she was 13. Her father was an analyst for The House, rising to head of Pasts Strategies for the Asia desk before quasi-retiring a decade ago. Yuko had been a natural recruit. The House had zero tolerance for nepotism, but sometimes talent didn't fall far from the tree. Relatives were allowed to join The House, but their family had to pay their salary and bonuses for the first two years before an independent committee would decide whether to keep the individual or cut them. There had been no dissent on keeping Yuko.

"Let's get out of here." I said to Yuko as the driver took my bag. Yuko led us out towards the limousine queue, her heels clicking confidently across the stone.

"I got stalked at LAX." I told her as soon as we settled into our car. "An unsolicited offer from a patsy for two sides of a trade. $26 million dollar Vietnam War option. Local frame. Back to '65."

"Shit..." Yuko pulled out her phone and calculated. "That could be 7% compound. That's probably a billion dollar past."

"I know."

"What's the other side of the trade?"

I lowered my window to sniff the Tokyo air, then turned to her and grinned. "A happily ever after."

Yuko scoffed, "And who's the patsy?"

"Some guy. An unknown. A San Francisco type. Sounds like a lineweaver tipped him off. Fucker was following me. Tried to rattle me. He wants us to tweak his past so that his mother loves him more or something. We'd need a late '70s, mid '80s capital block probably."

"Rural or urban?" Yuko asked.

"Sub-urban. I suspect."

Yuko sat back and weighed it up for a few moments. "It might work. It'd be at least 5% of your capital though."

"I know."

"Surely he's not going to do a one-to-one trade?"

"I think it'll cost us 10%. But I'd already decided to up the stakes anyway. So it'd be close to neutral on our base calculations. I was going to put that to Tatsuma tomorrow."

Yuko sucked air through her teeth, "He'll like that."

"I think it makes sense."

"Well that's good." Yuko grinned. "So which lineweaver tipped him off?"

"Curtis... I suspect. Maybe she thought she was doing me a favor. But it means our deal confidentiality's fucked."

"Someone's gone over our head."

"Yep."

"Could it be a trap from another fund?"

I blinked. I hadn't really thought of that.

"Try and get us to juice the wrong direction," Yuko continued, picking absently at her chin, "Push the other side of the trade then fuck us on the spill."

"I don't know..." I answered honestly. "Most managers are pretty settled on their Vietnam War positions at the moment though. The trade's attenuating nicely. There's a lot of entropy and most of the obvious pasts have been over-traded. So why try rumble us on such a narrow arbitrage? And in any case, I think the patsy was too transparent to be a good actor."

"Sounds like the men you date."

"Thanks."

"So how did Jim Morrison take it?" Yuko asked.

It took me a few moments to realize that she was asking about Marco. I had already compartmentalized him into a low importance drawer in the back of my mind. I thought about it: "He was just confused mostly."

"Hurt?"

"Confused. I think he believes that the world is fundamentally governed by love. Not by markets."

"Does he have a point?"

I had to look sideways at Yuko to confirm that she was serious. She looked back at me from behind her angular black sunglasses, her face inscrutable.

"Can love shape the past and the present?" I ventured, guessing at her meaning. She nodded. I thought about it. "Culture can dramatically alter the past. But the alterations are deeply chaotic.... It isn't well understood..." I offered lamely.

I tried again: "Look you'd expect that collective love can affect the past as it does the future, on some very large scale." I shrugged. "It's similar to the question of whether churches can be effective - or like... organized religion. And the answer is yes and no. They can be hugely impactful, but the impacts are non-linear and extremely hard to replicate, even if the church itself has become more cohesive. To *some extent* the weight of belief seems to be capable of refining the truth of the past, but because beliefs are so varied, even amongst zealots, the collective transition is almost impossible to game."

"But beliefs and thoughts can change the past?"

"Yes. Probably. But it isn't an easy way to make money so we haven't really looked at it."

Yuko nodded and turned back towards the Tokyo skyline, her glossy fuchsia-nailed fingers massaging her petite jaw. "Interesting."

Yuko was my unofficial protege of sorts. I was too junior to have a protege really, and she was only a few years younger than me, but her trajectory through The House had been very different to mine, and our organization has the sort of flexibility that nurtures and encourages productive groupings of minds - irrespective of formalities. Yuko was becoming my right hand.

"We need to discuss The Napalm Trade." I told her, bringing the conversation back to earth.

"Of course."

"How we're pitching it to Tatsuma."

"Ahh."

4.

The first time he had killed a man had been in Oruzgan. A squeeze of his finger had folded a human being like paper. And left this… dead shape in the dust. He may have directly killed a few others in Afghanistan: a spray of bullets into high grass at long range, a grenade round into a foxhole.

The second time he knew for sure he had killed someone, he had been fifteen miles outside of Aleppo with Turkish Peshmerga. Clearing a house and coming eye to eye with a Daesh fighter a heartbeat before he put three bullets into his chest. Ragged on the floor, the man had looked at him for four broken breaths, and then his eyes had gone silent, time seeping away and out of him.

He was on the Polish border now, trying to ensure that anger would provide the confidence for him to kill again. He knew that the fear would help.

"Yo Jimmy *mate*," Jesús yelled to him, "we need your dumbfuck Australian passport again."

Jesús was American. From San Antonio, though in Syria the YPG had thought his Mexican heritage might be Greek. So now everyone called him 'El Greco'. Jimmy preferred to call him Jesús most of the time though, because it sounded biblical. And El Greco sure as shit seemed to have a biblical rage in him.

The Ukranian attache had been expecting Jimmy and Greco's arrival at the border, but was proving meticulous with his paperwork. This was evidently frustrating Jesús. Jimmy was taking it in his stride. He turned back from where he had moved further up the road to get a better view of the defenses on this side: piles of raised earth wrapped in barbed wire and tank traps. They had already crossed a few lines of defense, but the main trenches and dug-in positions were apparently just ahead. The Poles were afraid that Russia was going to march through Ukraine and straight across their eastern border.

The attache was sitting at an old classroom desk out in the open. Some bored Polish guards sat in a hut a few meters further back.

"You will need sign International Legion contract inside the country." The attache said in rapid fire English, his accent unmistakable but his words precise. He took Jimmy's passport again and photographed it with a cell phone. El Greco handed Jimmy a stapled document. The attache continued: "Your commanding officer will collect signed contract and allocate pay."

"We know, we've seen the brief." Jesús insisted, he turned to Jimmy and waved his own version of the document towards him, "What are you going to do with all your monthly *hryvnia* Jimmy? How much is 6,000 hryvnia worth?"

"About 200 American dollars." The attache answered. "But this money will need to be held in account for you. We will not pay direct, because then Russia might think you mercenary, not volunteer, then - " he ran his index finger across his neck and made a choking sound. "But food, clothes, gun, bullets... we provide. But you are volunteer, not mercenary."

Jesús nodded. Jimmy glanced at their gear bags, they were bringing across body armor, scopes, nightvision, grips, magazines, batteries, radios, eight drones, a shit load of medical gear, and other tactical miscellany including a bunch of different currencies.

The Past Trader

He and El Greco sure as fuck weren't doing this for Ukranian money.

El Greco had called him two weeks earlier and pitched Jimmy on flying to Poland, crossing into the Ukraine and helping to train up some of their troops near the border. Teach them how to use javelin missiles to swat Russian tanks. It wasn't entirely clear to Jimmy who had roped Jesús into this adventure. El Greco was ex-infantry. A legitimate hard-arse who enjoyed cigarettes and eating a bit too much to cut it in special forces, but who probably had the equivalent of ten combat tours under his belt. Made most green berets just look green.

Jesús and he had more meaty paychecks waiting for them back in the states. Jimmy wasn't sure who was paying them. He trusted Jesús enough to not get stressed out about it. Probably CIA or some such. Maybe US mil. It wasn't at all clear to Jimmy that Jesús had ever truly left official duties.

The fact that the two of them had flown into Poland rather than Ukraine itself had elevated some of Jimmy's suspicions. Border tension had limited some flights but hadn't stopped them yet. This whole op felt very deniable. Jesús seemed confident that war was about to kick off, but Jimmy was skeptical. Tanks hadn't gone toe-to-toe in Europe since the second world war. This would be a Clausewitz style, Napoleonic fucking war of conquest. Jimmy's testosterone was salivating at the prospect, but he still didn't quite believe it would actually happen.

Jesús' phone rang, "Yo, this is Greco," he answered. "Ok, speak to me." He turned and looked at Jimmy. "1700. Ok." His tone of voice was official. Taking orders. "Copy that." He hung up and looked like he was about to say something to Jimmy. But cracked a grin instead and turned back to the official. "Yo Ivan, Egor, whatever the fuck your name is. Let's get this show on the road." He rotated his finger like a helicopter.

The man scowled at him. He sorted the documents on the table and handed them to the two men. "Walk across border," he pointed. "Show them passport. Good luck. Hope you don't get killed. Quickly."

El Greco slapped the man on the shoulder and he and Jimmy hoisted their gear bags and began walking towards the border. El Greco stopped when he was five meters inside the Ukraine: "Don't get killed *quickly*? Was that fucker wishing us good luck or bad luck?"

5.

The first past she had ever wanted to own was an English colonial trade from India in the 19th century. The arbitrage had a simple carry so she thought she could take a long position on South African gold in the '30s.

But she fucked up. She hadn't understood the market dynamics of Indian industrial machinery - sewing machines basically. The trade slipped. She wiped out 800 million dollars.

But the more haunting fact was that the GDP of a province of 200 million people was damaged in real terms by a quarter of a percent. She was able to resolve on the higher death rates of the time and knew that *statistically* she had probably just killed - in some sense - 25,000 people.

She wasn't completely clear on what that sense was. There was some faint substance to it. Some grain of reality in a sandstorm of the mind's eye.

She traveled there, to that province, and rode out in a tuk-tuk to an ancient factory that had shuttered probably 20 years before its time.

A beggar sat on a low wall of blasted concrete next to the broken frame of the building. He stared at her as she approached, camera and cap in hand.

He was a holy man perhaps, certainly an ascetic - matted hair and yellowed eyes. He smiled to open a vista of broken teeth and infected gums: "Krishna has come to look upon his necropolis. I see your form o' destroyer of worlds."

She glanced about behind her then realized that the man was blind. She sat down in the concrete dust beside him, facing the wreckage of her decision. "Death was not my intention here."

"Death and life - you think these binary?" He asked.

"I suppose that I see life as a ravelling together and death as a teasing apart."

"And this place - it has teased apart?"

"So it would seem."

"But this building is just a destination that once knew a different form." The man said carefully. "A block of riches that men dreamt would bring them more riches. Is it not just their dreams that have been teased apart?"

"Or annihilated."

"And what substance do you think these men were? Mere threads woven from the eternal?"

"Something like that." She answered.

"And each thread, governed by some weighted statistic?"

"Each thread."

He turned and grinned at her. A maniacal thing. Saliva glistened on the inverted peak of a lone incisor: "You are a frail imprint upon the infinitude. You are yet but a fragment of a potent form." He raised an open palm, "I do not diminish you out of a failure of imagination, or a belief that your status or shape are complete. But I *fear* you o' bean counter of the infinite. Because you only walk in one space."

She breathed out, then in, then out, and stayed sitting beside the man as the night fell through a ruddy dusk. They did not speak again.

The Past Trader

When the smell of flat bread, fresh in the cart of a passing hawker, eclipsed the chemical gradients in her nostrils, she snapped from her reverie and stood to buy food.

"Do you eat, o' many mouthed figure of the infinite?" She asked with as much sass as she could muster.

But he was gone.

6.

She was feeling tired after her flight to Tokyo but stayed awake until 10pm to hear the morning briefing out of New York. Yuko had joined her at the hotel for a working dinner in a conference room, and had only gone home thirty minutes earlier.

Tallie liked to stay at the Park Hyatt when she was in Tokyo. She told people it was because the location was convenient and the bath tubs were perfect, but really it was because she loved the film that had been shot there, *Lost In Translation*. It wasn't lost on her that she had more in common with Bill Murray's character than with Scarlett Johanson's. She cast the film to the television from her laptop and put it on mute in the background.

The morning briefing was The House's daily sermon. The consolidated desk would provide the lead overview, then each trading desk would give their analysis of the core pasts, presents, or futures that were moving markets. It was usually the deputy head of the relevant desk who would provide the breakdown. There were about fifteen minutes of briefings, then five minutes of pontificating from senior managers, then about ten minutes of discussion and Q&A. VPs like Tallie were expected to contribute to the Q&A portion about four times a year, though it wasn't exactly compulsory. Any more contributions than this implied that you were a showboat, while any fewer suggested that you perhaps weren't atop your brief.

Tallie knew she wouldn't be contributing today. Being on anything less than top form was an act of hari-kiri - ritual suicide. She ran her finger along her belly where a Samurai might make the two crucial cuts to gut themselves. She was half wrapped in a white silk kimono, lying on her bed on the 42nd floor overlooking the empire of light that was Tokyo. Her phone was on the nightstand set to speaker, blasting out a slightly tinny recording of Beethoven. She watched the clock tick to ten pm.

"*Good morning.*" The call began, it was Vance, deputy head of the London consolidated desk. "*The present is down. The NASDAQ by 1.2%. The S&P by 72 basis points. Primarily on concern over the Russian troops massing at the Ukraine border. There's speculation at both ends on Russian stocks. Futures are pricing in minimal bloodletting, falling less than 2%, while wheat prices have moved up 1.6%. We are trimming exposure and banking gains. Pasts are consolidating. The VMX is up 3%. There's huge interest in the Crimea Trade, and a lot of movement in The Indian MIG-29 Trade. We largely exited our position in the latter with a 316% return...*"

Tallie listened idly. She was waiting to see which managers would peak their head above the parapet.

A text came in from Yuko: [Shintaro wants to see you before Tatsuma. At 8am. Do you remember where he lives?]

"*...We think the impact on supply chains will be sharp but short lived...*"

[I think so.] Tallie replied, [The humpty dumpty house?]
[Exactly.]

"*...Greek shipping trades from the mid '70s have seen an interesting rerating. We think the price action is due to another fund making a significant trade. We are alert to any historical eclipses in tangential markets. We are carefully monitoring the situation in the Ukraine for opportunity...*"

[How much do you know about Napalm?] She texted Yuko, [About the chemistry I mean.]

[Not a lot. A toxic way to start a BBQ by most accounts]

[Definitely a challenge for rare steak.]

[You having second thoughts?] Yuko asked.

"*...We think a broader war would be an act of extreme financial irrationality. We continue to feel supported in our base assumption that the Russian political system is sufficiently financed...*"

[I always have second thoughts. And usually fourth and fifth thoughts. Not sure it helps.]

"*...We expect invasion of the eastern provinces, but we do not anticipate a larger invasion or an attempt to take Kyiv...*"

[That's why they pay you the big bucks]

"*...We expect that strategically consolidated greed will curb this conflict...*"

[I wonder if that's true.] Tallie replied.

[Why do you think they pay you?] Yuko asked.

[Probably because I stop thinking by the sixth attempt. You should get to bed.]

[Goodnight. Am I missing anything on the call?]

"*...We do not expect this to lead to an uncontained war...*"

[Absolutely nothing.]

The Past Trader

7.

Shintaro was the best lineweaver she knew.

Pasts were financial instruments, they weren't just ethereal concepts. For a past to be effective it had to weave a line between the anchoring event and the present via a hard edged aggregation of stocks, bonds, currencies, property rights, and options.

In theory the channels to events were infinite and stretched far beyond any so-called historical moment in time. Yet the lineweavers were the seamstresses of history, pulling forth threads from chaos and knotting them into clusters of analytical trading potential. It was a strange, subtle art, extraordinarily well paid for the limited few who were gifted at it. In day-to-day parlance they were referred to simply as "analysts", but Tallie preferred "lineweaver" as the more elevated sobriquet.

Shintaro's house was a strange assembly of concrete - like a cracked egg that had crystallized in the cracking - just off a side street in a middle class neighborhood of Tokyo. Shintaro watched her from up on his balcony as she approached, pulling slowly on a cigarette and letting the smoke flow evasively between his nose and mouth before vanishing into the morning breeze.

He didn't say anything to her but gestured that she should enter the house through the cherry red front door. The place was silent like a tomb. A peculiar row of paintings proceeded away from her down the corridor, each slightly smaller than the last. The effect made the space seem elongated like a rabbit hole. She looked more closely at the paintings as she passed them, they depicted a tall man beside a sailboat, dressed in western clothes but surrounded by women in kimonos. The detail was inverted, so the paintings got ever more precise as they got smaller and smaller. She climbed a stair that ascended awkwardly from a short passageway off the main hall. A white cat sat on the top stair. It hissed at her then vanished through a gap in the bannister.

The smell of paint was apparent by the time she was half way up the stairs. There was an atrium-like room of pale timbers and a slanted glass wall that looked out upon a distinctly Japanese landscape of bland white residential towers scattered across the greenery in infinitudes.

There were dozens of white canvases piled against the walls. Perhaps hundreds. All scrawled with the same Japanese character or *kanji*, either in black or in red. She was a bit shocked by the sight, because it implied something mad or maniacal in the ad infinitum expression of it.

Shintaro entered from the balcony and stood there watching her reaction with a defiant mixture of pleasure and embarrassment.

"What does that kanji say?" She asked.

"It means both lunch and dinner. Depending on the context."

She tilted her head as she looked at it, then glanced back at him. "You're fucking with me aren't you?"

A big smile: "Come down and I'll make tea."

They retraced her steps downstairs and walked through into a kitchen of green stone countertops.

As Shintaro made the tea, Tallie brought him up to speed on the state of play and the man at the airport.

"When I started at The House we had a name for a seller like that." He told her.

The Past Trader

"A patsy?"

"No, it's a little hard to translate - and it's crass - but we called them a *spooning man*."

"I don't get it."

"Because they can be on your side but still be in a good position to fuck you."

"Nice."

8.

El Greco and Jimmy were led into the armory by the Colonel. About 30 javelin missiles were stacked in black cases. Shoulder-mounted, man-portable, Russian tank killers. Jimmy had a nervous moment searching around the room for the CLUs - the Command Launch Units - the grips that contained all the optics and guidance systems, and without which the missiles couldn't fire. But he found those stacked behind the tubes. To his further relief, Jimmy also found a heavy-duty black suitcase that he knew would fold out into a training simulator. He opened it and checked the power. It was an old piece of kit, but it was working.

"Fucking perfect." He noted.

"Rock and roll." Greco agreed.

"Pretty rare to get a full set."

"Just about unprecedented."

"Are we ready to kill Russians?" The Colonel asked.

"Soon." El Greco nodded.

9.

The adhesiveness of basic Napalm is determined by the amount of rubber added to gasoline. As this mixture burns, an exothermic cascade of heat and light guzzles the oxygen from the air, creating a sticky flame. But the chemistry of Napalm can be modified by replacing the rubber with styrene - similar to styrofoam packaging - dissolving that in a solvent, then adding it to a petrochemical base.

Sold by Dow Chemical between 1965 and 1969, the profitability of styrene-enhanced *Napalm B* was suppressed by inferior distribution, a labor shortage in a key production market, a series of industrial strikes, and a warehouse fire in the spring of '66. As per our analysis, there was a very strong line implying that a drastic improvement in competition for that underlying business could rewrite the history of an iconic merger between two adjacent conglomerates in 1972.

We were clear on the upside from this trade - or as clear as was ever possible. We had thought about the angles, had lists of what could go right, and what could go wrong. We had modeled extensively on spreadsheets. Ultimately, we knew that we should end up with a more flammable napalm arriving on the market a decade earlier than previously.

While it was hard not to have misgivings about enhancing the deadliness of one of civilization's most lethal weapons to date, on the flipside, our analysis indicated that courtesy of that line being woven, major combat operations of the Vietnam War should end 60 days earlier - plus or minus ten days. So net net, this trade should preserve in the order of 7,500 lives. Perhaps as many as 15,000. Along with a tidy profit of between 10 and 30 billion dollars in the current frame.

We had gathered a pile of pictures from the time. Corporate group photos where the adults sat like school children. We wondered about their families, their offspring, their progeny. Whether certain threads of distant ancestry might be dissolved by our actions. It had never been entirely clear as to whether or not this truly happened. It seemed as though with family trees, the further you went out on the branches and beyond the extrema of knowledge, you came to a place where pasts merely flickered and danced in uncertainty. Vibrant lifetimes attenuated to vague shadows on the wall.

When she had first started working for The House she had often pondered whether a good historian and geneticist - meticulous in their family tree, and in the narrative of every second and third cousin, and step uncle twice removed - whether that person might be able to map each of those relationships to find uncleavable lines of DNA in the nucleus of being. But it turned out - or her conclusion at least - was that even a meticulous historian was still subject to the confusion of change. In many ways such a historian was a lineweaver - almost by definition.

But for a long time she hadn't understood how a biological map could fade and be distorted when it seemed as though it were the atomic and chemical formula for present existence. Of course the answer was obvious - biology wasn't quite what was taught in school. Today many analysts went so far as to attribute cancerous DNA mutations to cleaving pasts.

The Past Trader

Shintaro's office was an entirely functional space. Unlike the rest of the house, there was no art on the walls - no distractions - just tatami mats and a whiteboard.

Piles of paper and photos were loosely arranged on the floor with arrows on post-it notes going between them. Banthour Chemical had a place of pride in the center. All the reweavings were pointing to a far greater existence for this curious little minnow.

"It's the key to the trade." Shintaro told her, standing over Banthour's paper pile, and gazing down at it with intensity. "Banthour never quite figured out a performant recipe for napalm. Choosing instead to move into chemical flavorings and fragrances which only returned a modest 3% growth over ten years, prior to the chairman having a heart attack in the bath in 1975." He paused and scratched the back of his head, "Do you think Tatsuma will like this?"

"Yes. He will think it the perfect company. The profit line is so obvious."

"Are you sure that this is the sort of place that we should play in?"

"No." She answered honestly. "No, I'm not sure of that at all."

10.

Tatsuma was The House's most successful trader in all of Asia and a gold plated son of a bitch. Tatsuma had been stationed on Rostov's final desk in the '80s, and still advocated that ruthless, swashbuckling style of trading that was no longer in vogue with most of The House, but which was forgiven for generating extraordinary profits.

The House's investment thesis had shifted radically in the 1960s due to the breakthroughs in physics most commonly associated with Richard Feynman. In 1967 The House's most revered analyst, Igor Rostov, realized that Feynman's description of anti-matter explained something very deep about the world that the market wasn't aware of. Rostov proposed a way of leveraging that understanding for profit.

Feynman demonstrated that there are two equivalent descriptions for understanding anti-matter - which is the stuff that makes PET scanners in hospitals work - it can either be understood as matter with negative energy moving forwards in time, or as matter with positive energy moving backwards in time. Feynman showed that this was the exact same description. Look closely enough at the fabric of the universe and time loses its direction. Rostov realized that this meant that only the present truly existed.

Rostov and the Managing Director at the time, a man named Whitenby, set up The House's first Pasts Trading Desk in a trial of Rostov's thesis. Rostov's genius was to recognize that quantum uncertainty evaporates all chains of causation - there is no first mover because there is no first. The past does not exist as some definitive point. It is in a superposition - in all possible positions at once - and thus the state to which the past collapses is *malleable*.

Tatsuma was Rostov's last acolyte before the man died of cancer.

A crueler rumor was that Rostov died of Tatsuma.

*　　*　　*

Tatsuma had arranged seats in the Opera City Concert Hall. A vaulting triangular space of woven timber and ambuscading light. He arrived after the second bell. His face soured when he saw her, but he forced a smile and offered a precisely courteous bow. His suit was immaculate and his face was handsome though severely acne scarred.

"So Miss Dandieu" Tatsuma asked her in perfect and only lightly accented English, "do you enjoy the opera?"

"Yes." Tallie lied.

Tatsuma tilted his head, "I was told you hated it."

Now who told you that, she thought. "I'll admit that I prefer ballet."

Tatsuma laughed, an abrupt "Ha!" as though he had successfully trapped her. "And what do you despise about the opera?"

"I don't despise it. And I always like to experience new things. But in the past at least, I've found it a bit too... camp for my tastes."

"And ballet isn't?"

"I find that more distracting."

He summoned a waitress with a tray of drinks. "Champagne?" He asked.

She thought about it. "Sure."

She wondered if she should have chosen the soda water, but figured tonight was meant to appear like play, even if it was absolutely work.

Tatsuma took two glasses and handed her one. Tallie gave a slight bow to the waitress.

"So what have people told you about me?" He asked.

"That you're exacting on detail. That you don't suffer fools."

He barked his little laugh again, "I've heard similar of you."

"I didn't say they're not traits that I respect."

"Marius says that you're the most promising trader that he's ever trained."

Marius she realized. "That's generous."

"He also says that you hate opera."

"Ahh."

Tatsuma eyed her with a self-satisfied sort of a look.

"You opted to bring me somewhere that you knew I wouldn't enjoy?" She quizzed him.

"Yes. That is an adequate metaphor for the market." He sipped from his glass and eyed her forensically, "But no, *I* enjoy these performances, these are the most prized seats of the season, and I thought that your reaction would at least provide a little information. I would learn what you look like when you lie."

"I feel that courtesy can sometimes be more valuable than a mild deceit." Tallie explained herself.

Tatsuma gave the most deep smile she had seen so far. "Quite." He agreed. "I like gaining insight into an individual's discomfort if I am giving them nine billion dollars."

"Ten," she corrected him apologetically. "Or nine point nine technically."

"Oh?" He raised his eyebrows. "Let's negotiate on ten then. What's one hundred million dollars between friends?"

"The trade will carry less risk. Some extra '60s options appear to have become available. Their swap will require more capital, but the trade will become much easier. The downside will be better protected."

The bell chimed repeatedly to inform them and the other stragglers that the opera was about to start.

"We can discuss that in the intermission." He walked her towards the doors. "Marius is one of the best managers that I've ever worked with. I would hesitate before denying his protege, but that's not to say that I won't."

"That's reasonable."

"So what do they really say about me?"

"That you're a gold-plated son of a bitch."

He laughed, much more sincerely this time, a rumbling *ho ho ho ho*. "I've heard worse than that."

Tallie gave him a wry grin, "I haven't always been described warmly myself."

"No." He nodded. "Wear it as a medal."

They took their seats to the left of center at the front of the second floor terrace. The seats slightly surprised her. She had expected the best seats in the house. But then again, Tatsuma was an employee of The House, which meant that he understood value and was more than a little afraid of opulence.

"Have you ever heard of Toshihiro Watanabe?" He asked her.

"No."

"You won't have." He turned and looked at her closely. His acne pocks were dimples in the shadows. "As a child he was very terrible to me… And violent. Once I had enough capital I destroyed his ancestry. Meticulously. The town he was from, it was known for its pottery. A most delicate and meticulous application of Urushi lacquer upon a primeval native Jomon style. They are now extraordinarily rare. I have the most valuable collection of them in the entire world. And one day I shall destroy that too. You will find no mention - anywhere - of Toshihiro Watanabe."

"Why would you tell me this?"

"You are not shocked by the fact of it?"

"It seems a little -" she balanced her words on her tongue.

"Petty?" He suggested.

"No. *Indulgent*, I was going to say."

He laughed. "A reasonable assessment."

The lights dimmed.

"We must start the first act." He stated.

11.

The two women crossed a fizzing expanse of color, light, and movement. Languid male bodies in three piece suits and engorged pompadours perimetered the Pachinko parlours and pouted at girls in fuck me boots and teeny-tiny-skirts in shades of silver embedded with LEDs. Tallie and Yuko were in an edgier part of Osaka. Working boys and girls, and comfort companions of multitudinous stripes and sequins populated each corner and every alley. Bemused tourists traversed the technicolor with jaws agape.

Tallie and Yuko crossed a footbridge flanked by electronic billboard screens wrapping the skyscrapers on either side. Advertisements and pop culture - almost all in Japanese - erupted and dissipated in chaos and color.

"So what has Shintaro been teaching you?" Tallie asked Yuko, peering over the side of the bridge down into the rainbowed river of reflected light. She caught the unpleasant smell of decay and the sea.

"About trading?"

"About risk."

Yuko put her back to the water and propped her elbows on to the railing. "That risk is largely incalculable. That informal estimations are more valuable than misleading presumptions of accuracy."

"Hmmm." Tallie thought about it. "Sounds like a valuable lesson."

"I think I already knew it to some degree, but I've just been shocked by how instinctive Shintaro is. I expected him to rely on harder numbers."

"But how can numbers be hard if what they are describing is in flux?"

"I know. But I take comfort in false precision."

"We all do. Vast industries are shrines to that deceit."

Tallie had taken the Shinkanzen bullet train up to Osaka a few hours earlier. Yuko had needed to come here for personal business that she hadn't entirely explained. She had invited Tallie to join her so they could visit a curious temple and eat dinner at a restaurant that specialized in Fugu - poisonous blowfish.

Tallie had always liked Osaka. It felt edgier than Tokyo. More gritty and less meticulous. At the temple, Tallie was shown a statue completely covered in moss that was the last thing standing after getting bombed in 1945. Underneath the moss was a wrathful deity who supposedly converted anger into enlightenment. Yuko had faced the statue in silence then offered it a thin wavering candle.

"And how was the opera?" Yuko asked, taking Tallie's hand and inspecting it like a fortune teller. "It sounds like it was a positive meeting."

"It wasn't even a fucking opera."

"What?"

"It was a Noh play."

Yuko hooted with laughter. "Oh bloody hell, you poor thing... What did you think of it?"

"Just baffling." Tallie said, withdrawing her hand. "And it sounded horrible."

"I did wonder when you told me where you were headed. That isn't usually an opera venue you see?"

"But it was the Opera City Concert Hall?"

Yuko covered her mouth as she giggled. "The building is called the Opera City Tower but the opera usually happens in the National Theatre next door."

"Wow. Thanks for the warning. There I was expecting fucking Puccini, and instead I get half-cooked masked theatrics and wailing for two and a half hours. And Tatsuma continuously leering across at me with his shit-eating grin."

"Was he creepy?"

"No, I quite like him actually. The whole thing was a stitch-up to see how I'd react. The subterfuge and sheer guile of it was honestly incredibly impressive." She imitated his voice: "*Noh dramas are Japan's most rarefied art form. Ha! Ha! Ha!*"

Yuko giggled. "Rarefied about sums it up. Very esoteric. Very ancient. They're hundreds of years old. They usually tell of spirits trapped on the wheel of time."

"Well that's certainly how I felt."

"The spirits are between life and death you see. Did you at least like the costumes?"

"It was an avant garde Noh play. There were masks but no kimonos. Everyone was in white or black. Clapping and stomping. Occasionally shrieking. Baffling. Just baffling."

"Avant garde Noh?!" Yuko snorted.

"Shut up."

"But you closed the financing at least?"

"Not yet. But Tatsuma listened. I'm confident he's in. He suggested I leave at the intermission, but I stuck it out."

"He'll respect that."

"Or think I'm foolish and waste time."

"No." Yuko said confidently, "Staying was the right thing."

Tallie glared down into the shattering neon rainbows on the face of the water and tried to find the funny side of it all. It was still a bit too soon, but she grinned after a moment. "The wheel of time huh?"

"Samsara. The continuation of karma beyond birth and death. The cyclicality of all matter."

"Hmm, I missed that bit. Was too distracted by the wailing and stomping."

Yuko squeezed her in a hug. The gesture surprised Tallie in its intimacy. "What a thing to suffer through." Yuko said.

Tallie broke away. Only slightly awkwardly. She slapped Yuko on the shoulder and squeezed her arm, "Oh well, we'll bushwhack Tatsuma in New York and I'll pretend to take him to the boxing but actually put him in front row seats for *The Vagina Monologues*."

"I think you'd hate that even worse than he would."

"Yes. Probably. But if Tatsuma's taught me one thing so far it's that revenge is rarely practical."

12.

"Tallulah. To what do I owe this most profound honor?"

Kristen Curtis always emphasized her southern twang over the phone. It was the woman's not-so-subtle way of reminding her that even if Tallie could join any number of country clubs now, she would never be able to grow up in one.

"Tell me about your San Francisco guy?" Tallie asked her.

There was a pause over the line. "Who?"

"The guy you ambushed me with."

"I'm sorry Tallulah, who's that?"

"So you haven't been weaving lines for any tech bros?"

There was a pointed silence.

"I don't know what you're talking about."

"I was approached by someone at LAX. A cold call. He knew all about my deal. Played at being a commando but I think he's just a patsy. I'm trying to get to the bottom of how he knew about the trade."

"Why would you suspect me?"

"You have more knowledge than most people."

"Tallie I wouldn't try and rumble you like that." Curtis' voice softened. "I know that we're not friends. But I would hope that you agree that we respect each other."

Tallie thought about it for a moment. "I hope so too."

"Did he mention me?? Did this person mention me?"

"No. But he had a lineweaver do analysis for him."

"A *lineweaver*? Did it read like my work?"

"I haven't seen it yet."

"...And so if I'm your first guess, who are your second and third guesses for the culprit?"

"I don't know... I know that people talk, but this trade needs to fly under the radar at this stage."

"Tallie if I were you -" Kristen said with a sardonic tone, "- I'd start shaking the highest trees first, not my little mesquite bush."

"What do you mean?"

"Is someone of my stature going to leak a deal the size of The Napalm Trade? What would I have to gain from that? Why would I bet against The House? It's your big guys... Moorefield, Tastuma. *Tatsuma*, aren't you supposed to be running this trade with *Tatsuma*?"

"He's involved."

"Have you asked him if he knew the guy?"

"Not exactly. But I'm fairly confident that this man wasn't his associate. The style was all wrong."

"Oh, but it was right for me?"

"I'm sorry. There's just a very limited number of candidates who I can reasonably suspect of this."

"Have you notified Tatsuma that the trade might have been rumbled?"

"I'm trying to deduce whether it has been first."

"I think it's pertinent information that you might want to share with him." She said bitingly.

"I told him that there might be extra options from an unsolicited source."

"This commando's trying to trade you options?"

"Yes."

"What are these options?"

"Antecedents. 60's and 70's timeframe. Deep in the money."

She whistled down the line. "Sound tasty."

"Very. If they are what the patsy claims them to be."

"Do you know the size?"

"We think at least a billion in the current frame."

"Huh. Well that'd make your trade a lot easier, wouldn't it? It just about guarantees it."

"Yes."

"Hmmm… Sounds too good to be true. And this guy's rattled you has he?"

"Yes." Tallie admitted after a pause. "A bit."

"What a son of a bitch. Well… no Tallie, it wasn't me…" She sighed. "Are you still sufficiently armed to swap my '80s Imelda options."

"Absolutely."

"Great. Ok. Well if you resolve this mystery, I'm curious to find out who it was."

"So am I… Thanks Kristen."

The Past Trader

13.

No man's land was a few square kilometers around a busted hamlet and a truck depot with dug-in positions on either side. The Russians had fallen back to a sequence of new defensive trenches and the Ukranians had occupied a row of houses that offered the best elevation in the surrounding couple of klicks.

The truck depot sat along a crucial arterial road to the north. Five Russians lay dead in the frost there, scattered amongst the burnt-out trucks. They were in a half-life, rotten and frozen. You could find your way to the depot by smelling them.

For the past two nights El Greco's team had been staging out of a house 250 meters east-north-east of the bodies. Greco, Jimmy, the Canadian, and a British guy named Hooper had formed up with seven of the cluiest of the Ukranians. The local equipment was terrible. Cold war offcuts, interspliced with the occasional pristine pieces of combat gear donated by the west or from the corpse of a Russian Spetsnaz. Two of their guys didn't even have helmets.

The Russian's kit wasn't necessarily much better. The first wave that had been slaughtered here were poor kids out of Dagestan and yokels from the provinces. They had been sent into battle with combat rations that were years out of date. Jimmy and El Greco had managed to sneak up on a Russian position in the small hours with grenades, guided by the smell of the rancid latrine, and gambling on the expectation that a quarter platoon with severe food poisoning were probably an ineffective fighting force.

The following afternoon the Russians had gotten some revenge. Mortar rounds had smoked one corner of a house and knocked off one of their boys.

Jimmy and two others had carried the body back behind friendly lines while the others held the position. They waited out the day at the command post, then headed back beyond the wire at midnight.

Jimmy's little team approached the staging house in the dark. They paused a few meters before they would need to break cover and leave the laneway. Jimmy sought out a little piece of cord tied to the bottom of the fence. It was a rope that ran up to the backdoor and attached to a tuna can that would warn the rear sentry not to shoot them. He pulled it a couple of times, then felt the rope go tight. They still approached cautiously.

Hooper was on sentry by the window and he greeted them as they entered through the rear door. "Fuck me that rattling gave me a fright."

"Better than shooting us though I hope." Jimmy noted.

The others went into the middle room to try and catch some sleep. Jimmy headed up the stairs to the overwatch position.

"Ahh! Ares the god of war returns to us." Alexi said in his thick accent. He was a heavy-set Ukrainian, sitting upright on a chair, four meters back from a loophole that had been created by recent shelling. His faintly illuminated eye flitted across to Jimmy before returning to his rifle scope. He was scanning the fields beyond the house, a heavy caliber sniper rifle tucked into his shoulder and propped onto the table with a bipod. An elongated suppressor stretched from the barrel. The loophole - just a big hole in the wall really - gave a commanding view of the deathly landscape. A bed sheet had been strung up around Alexi to conceal his position. He would be very hard to see from the outside and he was very dangerous.

"That's funny." Jimmy said. "I don't feel so divine."

"God-like powers - they are usually overrated."

There was a window at the back of the room that looked back towards Ukrainian lines. The stars and moon cast monochrome. Jimmy glanced back in the direction of the command post then took off his webbing and helmet and put them against the wall.

"Do you think that's what Putin thinks he has?" Jimmy asked. "God-like powers?"

"I think that to be such an agent of death you need great detachment from moral consequences. Some amount of sociopathy or psychopathy. A fixed belief of yourself at the center of the universe. If you are convinced of that, you can do anything."

"Napoleonic shit."

"Yes. Napoleon also was an invader. And he went into Russia. But he made a big mistake. He waited too long in Moscow and got cut off from retreating across fresh land. He had to recross his earlier battle fields. Forced back through a no man's land like this. Down a memory lane of death with no food."

"You were a teacher right?" Jimmy asked.

"No. But I have PhD. In history."

"The history of Napoleon?"

"No. I researched the Polish-Lithuanian Commonwealth."

"Never heard of it."

"Ugh. You would not have. It was Europe's largest state in the 16th and 17th century. First unified in 1385. It became a federation of many cultures and elected kings."

"Sounds idyllic."

"Not so much. Not necessarily. But often peaceful. Prosperous mostly. In some ways it explains much of this conflict."

"Oh? How's that?" Jimmy asked.

"The commonwealth started between Poland and Lithuania, but it stretched all the way through Belarus, Ukraine. We were a different people long before the USSR."

"I thought ethnically, you and Russians were similar?"

"*Ethnically*? Well, what does that mean… Same blood stock?"

"Perhaps."

"You Americans are ethnically the same as English. Does that make you English?"

"I guess not. I'm Australian though by the way."

"Ahh, yes. The hopping god of war. The kangaroo born on Mount Olympus. But you are a warrior of the empire now. Are those missiles that you bring Australian?"

"No. But they might be."

"Yes they might. You are a vassal state."

Jimmy couldn't argue the point. "And how's happy hunting been?"

Alexi flexed his shoulders and shook his neck. He didn't say anything for a minute. "Violent…" he said after a time. "You would have shot your first man in ages past?"

"I've done some damage." Jimmy admitted, remembering a chest moving for four broken breaths.

"For me" Alexi said slowly, "it was only ever targets until recently. They are not the same thing."

"No." Jimmy agreed, "They are not the same thing."

"It is strange to want to hurt a person. The first man I killed, I felt so proud, then so ashamed. Like I wanted to hide what I had done from everyone. Even from my comrades. What would my mother think? Or my poor aunt?"

"They would think that you were defending the homeland."

"I was not. I was just killing a man. How is that defending the homeland?"

"The man was an invader."

"*Invader!* The man is a *boy*. A politician pawn. Far from the steppes with no horse."

There was a spotter's position in front of Alexi and to his side. Jimmy lay down on the grubby yoga mat and flicked on the nightsight that was there. It wasn't as good as Alexi's scope, but it was a decent piece of kit. He could find death with this.

No man's land emerged as a glowing saturated plane in two dimensions. A rural suburban sprawl of bucolic chaos. Serene catastrophe.

Jimmy remembered the first boy he had ever punched. He was perhaps 10 years old at the time. 11 maybe. And he had punched the much larger boy in the face. Repeatedly. Feeling this numb slap of flesh on his fists. And hitting the boy again and again. But receiving no reaction. Unable to diminish him.

A few years earlier than that - some memory from the edge of his existence - two older local boys had scared him, and he had run away and told his mother that they had hit him with a stick. And she confronted them and chastised them.

As a teenager Jimmy had enjoyed violence. But he had been deeply fearful of it too. He had tried to befriend bigger boys, older boys, dangerous boys. But then he had realized that even the toughest of these boys was nothing against a gun. Or a knife. Or a rock. And he had understood that there were weapons that he needed to know. That violence was not a kung fu film, or even a glass bottle against someone's head, not breaking, and bouncing off clumsily, then jarring his hand all the way up the elbow. It was the trigger pull. The weight of life and the consequence of subtle action. It was the headbutt into the nose and his teeth into the squid-like flesh of the cheek. Bite off the nose as he was trained to. The rush of blood and its chrome taste.

"Target. Twelve forty five. Three hundred meters." Alexi said quietly.

Jimmy greedily searched in that direction: a distinctly human blob, sliding across the expanse. The carnal thrill.

14.

They worked on the trade relentlessly. They were set up in the Tokyo office. Tatsuma was exacting on the details. Shintaro and he had evident friction that was glossed over in origami-like layers of precise Japanese courtesy.

Yuko was the first to arrive and the last to leave. This was the biggest deal she had ever worked on and her enthusiasm was considerable, though Tallie reflected that Yuko's late evenings were probably because Tallie - unofficially her boss - was usually the second to arrive and the second last to leave.

The Tokyo office was typical of The House. It was in the midst of the city's most expensive commercial real estate in Chuo, but in a second tier building with obstructed views. The ceilings were slightly too low, and while all the bells and whistles of a modern office were there, they were dated rather than top of the line.

Her desk was in the corner of the open office, looking out towards the Tokyo Sky Tree. Tatsuma had taken to working at the desk next to her. The Napalm Trade was just one of several deals he had on his plate, but seemingly most of his focus was here.

She realized that this was *mostly* because this was where Tatsuma saw the greatest potential upside, but she also got the impression that he was enjoying the caliber of Tallie's team and the process of mentoring them.

Tatsuma was schooling Tallie, taking apparent pleasure in passing his methodologies and frameworks on to someone as ruthless and calculating as he was. Well - that was what she hoped.

Less charitably, she wondered if he was just trying to learn the precise details of the trade so that he could fuck her.

Not sexually.

She hadn't received the faintest hint that he might be interested in fucking her sexually. It somewhat surprised Tallie. Perhaps slightly insulted her.

Even Shintaro had occasionally blushed in ways that told Tallie that beneath his obsequious Japanese exterior lurked just another man.

But Tatsuma was all business. He definitely might still fuck her commercially. Just not erotically.

Tallie had started to wonder whether this old enemy that Tatsuma had gone to such great lengths to destroy the past of - this Toshihiro Watanabe of the pottery dynasty - had perhaps been a romantic injury, more than the schoolyard bully she had first imagined. But it was pure speculation.

Perhaps he just wasn't that into her.

She had searched for Toshihiro Watanabe on the internet of course. And had discovered millions of results and references. But she suspected that none of these were the same man. Though that suspicion didn't stop her from spending a half hour memorizing the faces in the image search results... Just in case that information might one day prove useful.

One month into working together, Tatsuma invited her out to lunch.

The two of them changed subway trains twice and traveled together in near silence - neither of them putting great store in small talk.

The Past Trader

He took her to a tiny restaurant in a downmarket part of Tokyo that she had never been to. A chef stood behind a tiny counter with only five bar seats. The sole patron was a little old lady in a kimono, drinking beer and eating sashimi. She didn't even glance at them.

The chef and Tatsuma exchanged pleasantries in a way that implied that they knew each other, though most of the Japanese they spoke was lost on Tallie.

Tatsuma ordered superb sashimi. Pale toro that dissolved on the tongue.

"Why have you *failed* to obtain this lineweaver's analysis?" Tatsuma asked harshly and out of the blue.

The censure surprised her. "I have pushed for it." She told him, "We're the buyer here, but the seller doesn't appear to be motivated by the money. Our leverage isn't proving as strong as I hoped -"

"Then find other ways." Tatsuma glared at her. "If you expect to give this man billions of dollars in cash and options, then he needs to come to the table. First you tell me he is desperate, but now you can't get him to cut your deal. We are not buying fruits from a stand. You are taking too long, and we should be acting more quickly! Either we proceed or we don't."

Tallie nodded. She thought about arguing the point, but knew it would just antagonize him. And furthermore she knew that he was probably right. She shared this particular frustration.

"This is too big a deal for you." Tatsuma said coldly, "I think you're going to lose me a lot of money."

Tallie put down her chopsticks. She could feel sweat breaking down her back. "This deal is what it is. We are not operating with perfect information. We are riding market forces. We are maneuvering this trade as we are able. We have parameters for completing the trade without these options, or for including them. It isn't perfect but -"

"You're not thinking about this the right way!" Tatsuma barked, "There's something blocking your mind. You're too focused on making money. Money is not important - the uncertainty is. You need to recalibrate your thinking. I do not have the time to be this patient with you."

Tallie felt her face reddening. "...I appreciate the mentorship that you're providing me. I'm sorry that I'm a slow learner."

"You're a smart woman. But you are overconfident. Your lineweaver is a good analyst but he is not a great investor. Do not put too much weight on his decision trees and flow charts. Do not put too much weight on your spreadsheets and projections. The market is all of the present."

He barked each syllable, and she glanced at the chef and the other diner, who were both studiously looking elsewhere.

"The present will decide your Napalm Trade." Tatsuma continued sharply, "It is indifferent to your hopes and aspirations. It is indifferent to your data. You must change your thinking."

Tallie was taken aback. She hadn't expected a lashing. She wasn't entirely sure of the cause. But she knew that it was starting to look bad that she hadn't managed to obtain the mystery lineweaver's analysis. Tatsuma was suspicious and he was threatened by a very large risk.

She wondered at the degree to which Tatsuma's behavior here was driven by fear. What was he afraid of though? Nothing had ever given her the least sense that the man was a slave to loss aversion. But loss aversion and greed were very similar sides of very similar coins.

No, she recognised, she simply hadn't been doing a good enough job.

"I will work harder Tatsuma-sama. I am sorry that my performance has fallen short of your reasonable expectations of me. I will redouble my efforts to deliver you the results that you are owed."

He looked at her closely, then nodded once curtly. The House didn't congratulate you for great work. It always expected it.

He turned back to the sushi chef just beyond the counter, and rattled something to him in Japanese then laughed.

She felt a flush of embarrassment, but realized it was probably small talk.

Tatsuma paid the bill then stood and waited for her to stand. He bowed to the chef and they left the restaurant: "*Arigato gozaimashita*".

They returned to the office without saying another word.

15.

A call came in from Vance on the London desk. She was a little surprised to see his name pop up on her phone, though the two of them went way back.

"Tallie! Darling, how are you?"

"Hello Vance."

"Your Napalm Trade - someone's getting very muscular around the periphery I'm afraid."

She had pulled Vance in on a few of the details and he had helped her to get positioned for the trade. He didn't know everything but he knew a lot.

"I've been monitoring movements in some of your early positions." He continued, "It looks to me like another fund might be trying to get set up. I don't think they quite know what you're up to, but they're taking some pretty good guesses."

"Shit…" Tallie said.

"The volumes aren't too bad yet - the prices haven't changed dramatically. But there's mischief in the air, you know?"

"Thanks, I really appreciate the head's up."

"No, that's ok, I'll send you through a few data points. Are you near your email?"

"Always. Opening it now."

She went to her email app and found Vance's note at the top of her inbox. He had sent screenshots of daily trading volume on related ancestors. There was an uptick, that was for sure. But it was sporadic. It was like the buyer knew some of the companies involved but didn't know the way that they were going to be used, or which way The House was betting.

"These idiots could get burnt with some of this." Tallie observed.

"I was thinking the same thing."

"Interesting. Any way you can snoop out who this is?"

"I'm on it."

"Thanks Vance."

"There's two other things." He said. "First, I don't want to alarm you, but you're probably going to get a call from security today - there's been a wide spectrum attack on your accounts and passwords. These things happen, but the coincidental timing makes me nervous."

"Interesting. How'd you hear about it?"

"Grapevine."

She considered pressing him for more specifics, but knew she would probably need more favors down the line. "...I see. Ok. And the second thing?"

"Ahh yes! *Darling*! When-oh-when are you finally moving back to London? I miss you. Let's go to Annabel's. Get a cocktail!"

Tallie smiled. She and Vance had shared a few fleeting rendezvous over the years. It had started long ago, and was totally illicit and a dangerous violation of the rules of The House. But in both of their opinions it was more or less harmless - they were quite disengaged and certainly weren't the first or the last employees of The House to have wound up in each other's beds after a late night.

"That would be nice Vance. I'll be fully moved back in a few weeks."

"Marvelous!"

"How's… Lucinda?" Tallie asked, guessing at his girlfriend.

"Ahh. Lucinda." He paused.

Correctly guessing at his girlfriend Tallie noted.

"She's… good." He continued slowly.

"Great. Why don't you invite her?"

Vance laughed. "Can't get much past you hey Tal'?"

"You might say that, but it seems that plenty of people are getting plenty past me at the moment."

*   *   *

Tallie crossed the office to Yuko's desk and told her about the mystery buying and the security breach.

"I don't like any of this." Yuko remarked.

"No, nor do I." Tallie agreed.

"I would like to think that this is another fund, but there's something too… cozy about it all. There seems to be a familiarity with our methods, even if they're not clear on how we're playing the trade. I don't like it."

"But who would intervene against The House?" Tallie pondered aloud. Thinking again about one of the many things troubling her.

"A scorned government perhaps?" Yuko suggested, "Otherwise it would need to be a tier one fund surely. But this feels more like an inside job. Someone inside The House."

"Maybe." Tallie conceded with a sigh, "Have we learnt anything more about this fucking patsy's antecedents? I don't understand why he was in such a hurry when he approached me but now is jamming things up."

"I heard from him again." Yuko grinned and opened a document on her computer. The three screens in front flooded with charts and market data. "We now have the full specs on *all* his antecedents, they're as good as we dared to hope. I'm just cross-checking their veracity with our assumptions then I'll share a summary with you and Shintaro. I won't cc Tatsuma yet."

"Yes, don't. That's good."

"But the fucker's still being very reluctant with his lineweaver's analysis. He insists that he needs to get permission. Look."

Yuko opened her email and Tallie read it over her shoulder. The patsy had written:

> *Can you give me more details of how you will be making the trades and what the second and third order effects might be? I would appreciate feeling more comfortable with this.*

> *As I have repeatedly told you, I have asked the lineweaver for permission to share their document. I have just asked them yet again on your behalf. I'm sorry for the delay and I'm not trying to obfuscate. But I made an agreement when they gave it to me, and I do not yet have permission to share. I'm sorry. I hope that permission is coming.*

The Past Trader

Attached you will find the full and complete details of my assets. I hope this is sufficient for now. Please get back to me re. the usage of my assets when they are sold.
Fred

"*When they gave it to me...*" Tallie pointed out, "So it wasn't a simple work-for-hire then."

"Doesn't seem to have been."

"That's interesting."

"I get the sense that the patsy might... that while he doesn't know exactly what we're going to be doing with his options, I feel like he might be having -" Yuko studied Tallie's face carefully "- ethical misgivings."

"How luxurious that must be for him... And how are you feeling about it all?" Tallie considered Yuko.

The woman shrugged. "I'm still finding my bearings when it comes to the morality of modified causation."

"Aren't we all." Tallie agreed.

"Who can you discuss these hacks and skullduggery with? What if this is coming from inside The House?" Yuko asked. "Should you take it to Tatsuma?"

"No. I have a better idea." Tallie needed to speak to Marius.

16.

Jimmy met Anya at the checkpoint she was manning. He only glanced at her at first, despairing to see yet another schoolboy wearing a military uniform. But Anya looked up and Jimmy saw the most beautiful eyes that he had ever seen.

He looked away and pretended to check his weapon.

His unit had slouched in an hour earlier. Exhausted. Beat to shit.

Russian artillery had landed a little too close and his ears were still ringing. *Traumatic brain injury.*

They were lucky to have survived.

Jimmy tasted fear in his mouth, but it wasn't the Russians this time.

His mind rushed with potential strategies for approaching her. He had learnt a long time ago that he didn't give a fuck if he made a play at a girl and it went nowhere. Even being humiliated or sneered at was never - *never* - as bad as the feeling that the chance was there but that you didn't take it.

He decided to approach her directly. She clutched a clapped out AK-47. He tried Ukranian for hello: "Pryvit. Hi."

"Hi." She said. "You're foreign legion."

"It's that obvious?"

"I see your badge."

He looked at the trident on his shoulder and at the scythe-wielding reaper on his chest webbing in turn. "Yeah - oh yeah, of course."

She smiled at him. A little of her tinted hair poked from under an antique combat helmet. Her eyebrows were messy, but in a high fashion sort of way. He had never seen such a beautiful woman fighting a war.

"How long have you been a soldier for?" He asked.

"Since February. I'm from Odessa."

"God. I respect that you've wanted to stay and fight."

"I respect that you wanted to come and join us."

He nodded, lost for words.

"Where are you from?" She asked.

"I'm Australian. Originally."

"Oh!"

"But I've lived in America for a long time."

"Wow. I've always wanted to go to both of those places."

"Maybe we can take you to them. Your English is very good."

"I lived in the UK when I was 18. I worked as a nanny. I wanted to stay, but my mother..." she trailed off.

"Your family, are they out?"

"Out of the Ukraine? Some. Others... no. Maybe. I... I don't know."

He nodded, not knowing what on earth to say. "Are you billeted nearby?" He asked.

"Yes."

"Do you have a boyfriend?"

She laughed. "A boyfriend?"

"What's the Ukranian for boyfriend?"

"*Khlopets.*"

"You have one of those?"

"No. I think it would be strange to have a boyfriend in this violence."

"Yes. Probably." He conceded.

"Are you a violent man?"

"Yes."

"I never used to like violent men. Life has taught me differently."

She looked at his rifle. "And you are special forces?"

"Sort of. Yes. But I'm mostly training fireteams here. My role now is more infantry."

"But you are going on specialist missions?"

"Yes. Sometimes."

"Will you train me?"

"What training have you had?"

"I was given this." She held up her rifle awkwardly. "Shown how to point and how to shoot it."

"I will definitely train you." He promised.

"When can we start?"

He checked his body and felt the fatigue there - a weight at the back of his eyes. "I need to get a few hours rest. But I'll be here and away from the front for a few days. My ears have been damaged and I need to let them heal, and I'm going to be doing some planning work."

"After training can I join your team?"

"No."

"You think I am afraid of danger?"

"I don't get that sense." He answered honestly.

"Then why could I not join your team?"

"You don't have enough experience. Everyone in my team has had at least one year in the military."

"I see."

"Do you have friends around here?" He asked. "Like you - who I could also train?"

"Yes. Everyone here needs to learn to fight I think."

"Gather whoever you can. I have a Canadian friend with me from my unit - a very good soldier. He will also help. 7am tomorrow. We will meet... where should we train?" He asked her.

"There is a football stadium. A small one." She pointed up the road. "Where we learn to shoot our guns."

"I'll need to speak to your commanding officer."

"Yes, he is over there." She pointed towards a sandbagged position further along the road.

"Ok. Do you think you will all be able to meet at the stadium tomorrow at seven?"

"Yes. We will be there."

"And you need to tell your guys that we are a serious outfit who have zero time for go-pro fantasists and social media wannabes. I catch anyone using their phone and they're out."

"Alright. I will pass the message."

"Ok. And what is your name?"

"Grigori."

"Grigori. Is that your first name?"

"No."

"And what is your first name?" He smiled.

"Anya."

"I'm glad to have met you Anya. I hope that I can help you."

"You are helping me. You make me feel braver. I am glad you are in town for a few days."

"Every minute of training you get will be valuable. But it will only be a few hours and not enough to prepare you for real combat. But it will hopefully be enough to help keep you alive."

"I know that."

"Just try to get more training. Keep practicing. And stay in a defensive role until you're ready. Don't volunteer for the front. That way you can do more good once you're needed there."

She gave him a patronizing look.

"How old are you Anya?"

"24."

24. Jimmy felt crushed by it. It was one thing to see men dead. But to see yet another young woman - a pristine orchid like this girl, pulped between a hollow point and gunpowder...

That morning they had come upon a Russian tank many days dead.

Looking for intel they had tried to pull the bodies from the wreckage and a femur had come away in his hand.

Anya squeezed his wrist slightly and broke him from his thoughts. Her eyes probed his. "This isn't your first war is it?" She asked him.

He shook his head.

"Does it get easier, the better you know violence?"

He shook his head again. Then hesitated, "You can use it as a weapon. It doesn't get easier but it can become... more constructive."

She seemed to understand. "I'm not looking for someone to protect me." She said after a few moments.

He tilted his head, took in her wilfulness. "I'd love for someone to protect me." He grinned. "But I gave up on that long ago. I will help you to protect yourself."

"And I will try to protect myself. And perhaps we can try to protect ourselves together."

"For a while."

"Yes." She agreed, "For a while."

17.

Sydney was too far from the shimmering center of it all to be an acceptable place to live. Or that was what Tallie had always thought. Marius had been based here for 35 years. Enamored to the sun and the sleepy nature of the place. *Sleepy* wasn't necessarily the right word, but there was a certain *sameness* that characterized all smaller cities - a finite horizon line. There was none of the infinite improbable chance that a megacity offered.

His house was on the southern edge of the harbor. Usually it looked across a sapphire paradise leapt over by a brutal iron bridge that somehow seemed weightless. But today the city was lost in mist and the harbor was brown. The very crest of the bridge floated in the cloud. It had been raining for weeks.

Marius' hundred-or-so year-old house was wrapped by a porch, and they sat out on the edge of it under the awning, on an ornate cast iron table and chairs. His dog slept at his feet.

"How's your son Marius?" She asked him.

He glanced at her and she caught the pain in his eyes. He sipped his coffee carefully. "I haven't heard from him for a while, but I suspect he's in the Ukraine."

Tallie's eyes widened. "What would he be doing there?" She asked, but Tallie knew exactly what he would be doing there...

"It's a war." Marius said simply, "It's the sort of war he's always looked for. Always hoped for."

Tallie had met Jimmy three times. The first instance had been many years earlier when he had just returned from Afghanistan. He had had this... hunted look. She could see the anger in his knuckles. At his father's prompting he had taken her out for a very awkward drink at a bar beside the harbor. Some harmless drunks had looked at Tallie a little too closely, and Jimmy had taken affront. She had stopped him from ripping their throats out. Barely.

A week later Jimmy had knocked out a guest at the wedding of one of his best friends from the army. He had ended up on charges that Marius had managed to bury. She was told that the provocation had been non-existent.

The second time she and Jimmy met was in New York five years later. He was in America for reasons she couldn't quite ascertain and that he wasn't interested in divulging. He had looked leaner. More vicious somehow. It was as though the crumbling edges she had seen the previous time had been baked into place. In some deeper oven of hardship. He wore a Rolex and Gucci sneakers.

The third and most recent meeting was much the same. But Ferragamo on his feet and Hublot on his wrist.

"How's your father Jimmy?" She had asked him then.

Jimmy had shrugged. "He's still Marius."

*　　*　　*

"When's the last time you heard from him?" She asked Marius.

"A few months ago. A cryptic email. He said he might be off the grid for a while."

"Before the war started?"

"I wouldn't be surprised if he was in the vanguard."

The Past Trader

Tallie sipped her coffee. Over the years Marius had given her a patchwork of details of his son. Marius was not a man who sustained failure. In net effect Marius had told Tallie that Jimmy was the greatest failing of his life. He had never said it in quite so many terms. But he had communicated it. Repeatedly. Subtle shakes of the head. Meandering stories that came to a cliff's edge and broke off.

"When he was a boy, all he wanted was for me to take him camping. Of course I hate camping. There were a few weekends when I probably could have made it happen. Perhaps he would have learnt how miserable it can be. Maybe he would have…" Marius sipped from his coffee again.

She knew that it was an incredible act of intimacy for Marius to let her see this side of him. It was the only subject where he wasn't ruthlessly concise and devastatingly insightful. Jimmy had been raised by his mother who had despised Marius, eschewing both him and most of his money - limiting Marius' contact and his influence upon the boy. It was crystal clear to Tallie that Marius should have tried harder.

"He told me he caught up with you in Los Angeles a while back?" Marius asked, changing the tone.

"Yes." Tallie remembered, "Six months ago. We went to dinner. He didn't say much. He's still living on the East Coast. But… travels. A lot. He never tells me any details. He looks like he's living well. He is very fond of you, you know?"

"That's kind of him. He never had a sister, but I think he would be interested in you romantically if it wasn't for the fact that you're a hundred miles out of his league."

Tallie couldn't help but blush. She gulped her coffee to hide her face in the mug.

Marius looked at her closely, he had anticipated that his words would have this effect and was amused by it. His grin turned serious again. "I would be incredibly disappointed in you if you ever got romantically involved with my son. Which isn't to say that I don't love him, it is just that…" he trailed off with a grunt.

"So tell me about your trade." He prompted.

"What do you already know?"

"You're bundling antecedents. Aggressively shorting residual industries. Taking huge longs on some very weak ancestors. It seems like an exciting trade."

"It will be my biggest."

"I am pleased for you."

"There are contingent options though. They're on the table but we haven't closed them. They modify the trade a lot. Dramatically scale the upside. Marginally increase the risk on the downside. We've been offered them by an unverified source who ambushed me out of nowhere on the basis of some unknown lineweaver's analysis. This guy is maximally cagey. He's refusing to share that analysis and we've been pestering him to see it. There's a lot of trading activity happening that looks like someone is stalking out our battlefield. There was also an attempt to hack me… but that may have been unrelated."

"Can you make the trade without this analysis?"

"Yes, almost certainly."

"But you're fearful that someone's trying to fuck you?"

"More or less."

The Past Trader

Marius stretched boredly. "Tallulah you've been in this game long enough to know that the past never offers us perfect resolutions - we don't get happily ever afters or things tied neatly with bows. Or... *closure*, as they say."

"I know that."

"The House is a greedy place at its core. By its very essence. You're never going to have perfect insight into all of the competing agendas. You either work within the informational uncertainty or you hang up your boots."

"Nothing's ever certain." She recited.

"Nothing's ever certain. But The House always wins."

"But what if I get ambushed?"

Marius scratched the tip of his nose. "How bad could the downside be?"

"Financially? Five bil. Eight if things get really horrible."

"How do you weight that probability?"

"Under ten percent."

"Hmm. And the likely upside?"

"Three to ten X."

"Not bad. How hard is the *choice*?"

She smiled sadly. She had known that Marius would understand this. That he would see through her and cut straight to the real reason that she had traveled so far for his counsel.

"It's difficult. If we've got our lines tangled or have misunderstood the spill, there could be... bad - severe - consequences."

"I presumed by your nomenclature that your design for this trade did not presage happy outcomes for all."

"My nomenclature?"

"You have called it *The Napalm Trade?*"

"Oh." She said, "No, Yuko Matsumoto came up with that. Though it isn't especially original given it's more or less the heart of it."

"Mmm of course she did. And what are her compunctions?"

"I think she's willing to defer to me for her morality."

"Tatsuma loves the trade. I spoke to him last night."

"I never realized you two were so friendly."

"Mutual respect." Marius said simply. "He's not as bad as his reputation... Though his reputation is very dark indeed."

"So I've noticed." She shifted uncomfortably, "When a trade goes wrong, do you think that those people die Marius?"

"Die? I think that certain chains of causation unravel. Others fill the breach. The state of the present has too much nuclear density to shift dramatically. You kill ghosts and shadows, not people. But certainly the entropic chains alter. That's my working hypothesis in any event."

"But what of suffering?"

"I think the best you can do is try to act in the hope that most of your actions will diminish suffering, but of course compromise governs our every choice. Rarely can we choose good, much less the greater good. Nor do we usually get options for the lesser evil. In truth rarely do we ever choose anything. We just live with our compromises."

"Do you really think that's enough?"

Marius considered her. "Alternatively? Don't - play - the - game."

"Yes, but what else would I do?"

"Whatever you turn your mind to." Marius leant down and scratched his dog behind the ear.

"It seems clear to me that this trade will have adverse outcomes." She peered into the bottom of her coffee cup. "But great profit."

"My expectations lean in the same direction."

"Is profit worth it?"

Marius looked at her strangely. As though she had started reciting poetry in Cantonese or Finnish. "Profit is just your mark." He said to her eventually. "The money itself is irrelevant. The money became irrelevant for you long ago."

"I know." She said.

"But the scorecard still counts?"

"Yes."

"It's hard enough to beat the markets. In pasts trading we're not just trying to beat the market, but time itself."

"Yes."

"If there's ever been a greater test of human will and human brilliance I have not heard of it. Time humbles each of us - but profits only the very best."

Marius picked up a stick from beside his chair and flung it out for his dog. The animal lifted its head, stretched its back, and loped after it slowly, then bit into it and the mud beneath with its slobbering mouth. "At the end of the day we're all just organisms chasing baubles. So make your choice."

*　　*　　*

She had first been introduced to Marius when she was 19. She had just finished college. A sequence of scholarships for gifted under-privileged. She had completed a masters in theoretical physics.

Cathy Baubach, her favorite professor, had asked her to meet for lunch one day, and told her she had someone important to introduce her to.

Marius had arrived wearing a blue three piece suit with a ruby silk handkerchief tucked rakishly into the breast pocket. She had never met such a rarefied, kind, old gentleman.

"Tallie, this is Marius. He works for a company you might have heard of –" The professor had then given a flash history of The House, describing it as a financial octopus, its many tentacles reaching far and deep.

Marius sat there with a slight smile on his face, studying Tallie as he half listened to Professor Baubach.

Tallie had worn her best outfit that she owned at the time, and the only thing that seemed slightly appropriate: a hideous white cotton dress from Abercrombie and Fitch, fake leather brown boots that crested the top of her calves, and an ill-fitting blue blazer from a Goodwill. If you squinted she looked ready for a day at the polo.

"I'm sure that you've always thought that a career in finance is much less interesting than the secrets of the universe." Marius began, "And I'd forcefully agree with you in most circumstances. But what you perhaps don't realize with investing is that the best of us –" she had noted the implied ego in this statement and it immediately tweaked her curiosity, "- have to be deep across a vast array of technology and sciences. More importantly, there are trading strategies that dance far at the edge of what we understand -"

"High velocity quant trading?" Tallie interrupted.

Marius laughed. "No, far more complicated than that! The best of us have some sort of an instinct for it. Something that's almost impossible to train and that goes beyond mere precocity of intellect and far beyond what can be modeled on a spreadsheet in Microsoft Excel. Somehow that -" he pointed at her head then tapped on his own, "- can ravel together extraordinarily complex disparate lines of reality - of time, and experience, and knowledge - and devise trading strategies that generate tremendous profit."

Tallie had folded her arms skeptically.

"If you want to get into this game for the money," Marius continued, "then yes, you might make a bit. But you will not be successful. If you want to get into this game to be the best in the world in a discipline far grander and more complex than any Olympic pursuit - or any Nobel prize - then you should come and work for me."

Marius sat back, folded his hands on the table and continued to study her. Tallie looked across at Professor Baubach with confusion on her face. "This is a job interview?" She asked.

"The most interesting job in the world I promise you." Cathy said apologetically. "I worked for Marius for a little while. I frankly didn't have what it took to be a great trader. I realized that early on. There are... skills needed. A mentality more than anything. A flexibility of understanding. An attitude to failure. To complexity. To incompleteness. To be able to balance all of those things and take actions that get it right. You can be correct about sixty percent of the time if you're Marius. Fifty percent if you're good. My number was probably closer to forty."

"You're too hard on yourself." Marius told the professor.

"I'm honest." Cathy said simply. "The job was too complex for me, and I lacked the requisite mentality."

"I don't understand. This trading strategy that you're describing, how could it possibly be so complicated?" Tallie asked.

Marius picked up a menu from the table. "We should get something to eat. I have a long, very surprising thing to explain to you."

Tallie frowned. Marius perused the menu for a few moments then lifted his eyes. "I don't have all the answers Tallie. And there will be things I will tell you that will be deeply unsatisfactory. And those are exactly what I hope will get you hooked." He grinned and returned to the menu.

"I think I feel like the fish." Professor Baubach said.

The Past Trader

18.

When she stayed in Sydney, Tallie preferred a hotel that jutted into Sydney Harbor along an old timber pier, located in a suburb with the extraordinary Aboriginal name of Woolloomooloo. The rooms had the original beams and struts of the pier carved through the center of high ceilings. A skyline of surprising vitality and angular skyscrapers punctuated the view. Beneath it the harbor reflected an inky vision of emaciated light.

The building had two sides, the "Pearl Harbor" side that looked over a naval base of warships and antiquated aircraft carriers, and the "Saint Tropez" side of bubbling restaurants, self-conscious laughter, and clinking champagne flutes. She had first met Charlotte down there panhandling years before. Sitting on the boardwalk in front of an elite restaurant. The woman's nose in Dostoyevsky in a way that suggested that she wasn't taking her panhandling all that seriously.

Tallie had recognized Charlotte as an Aboriginal woman without quite understanding what that meant. When she was a child, Tallie had read some of the history of this country - abridged versions with two-dimensional depictions of the past. Black and white histories that described colonizers with rippling chests adding rose bushes and order to an uncouth wilderness where the black men and women were more like dangerous beasts.

Even then in her youth, Tallie had been innately skeptical of any narrative that sharply defined the abstract that she presumed history to be. Marius insisted that the contemporary local culture had improved in recent years, and that the 60-odd thousand years that Australia's native peoples had dreamt in this place was slowly being remembered for the remarkable legacy that it was. Tallie hadn't yet seen great evidence of this though.

The people of this land were ancient in a way that no others were, and they therefore understood time far more robustly than any other culture that Tallie had ever encountered. She supposed it was because they had been given a lot longer to think about it.

"Hello, I'm Tallie." She had first introduced herself to Charlotte, years earlier, intrigued by this lean and unkempt woman sitting on the wharf in front of aggressively affluent diners, and two thirds of the way through *War and Peace*.

"Tallie. Is that short for something?" Charlotte had looked up from her book, her voice croaking from decades of cigarettes. Trailing whiskers dotted her chin.

"Tallulah."

"You should stick with Tallulah. Your name is as old as time."

Tallie had searched her purse while she thought about that. "You have a nice view. Have you been here long?"

"I was, am, and will be here." Charlotte had said plainly. "There's no beginning or end."

Tallie had paused her search for cash and looked at Charlotte more clearly.

"That's a perceptive thing to say."

"It is what my people understand."

"Will you tell me more?"

This began their friendship.

* * *

The Past Trader

Charlotte hadn't been panhandling at her usual place when Tallie arrived in Sydney that morning. So after visiting Marius, she returned to the hotel then walked a few streets back to Charlotte's place - a poky old Woolloomooloo cottage, damp with terrible light. Tallie had bought Charlotte an elegant floor lamp a few years earlier and was itching to get the mold fixed.

The house was perched at the end of a row of government housing. Empty beer bottles and a scorched teaspoon littered the stoop and the tiny balcony. Tallie knocked on the glass pane in the door. Silence. She knocked again and listened more attentively, then poked her head around the nearby window. A heavy curtain stopped her from seeing very much.

As she walked back to the hotel she tried Charlotte's phone but it went straight to voicemail. Tallie tried calling one of Charlotte's daughters, May, a lawyer in the city.

"Hello, May speaking."

"Hi May, it's Tallie here. One of your mom's friends. She gave me your number a long time ago in case I couldn't find her."

"*Tallie?*"

"Yes. I used to be based in California, but come to Sydney every couple of months. I've known your mom for a few years."

"Oh. You're the one who bought mum that lamp aren't you?"

"Yes."

"I thought she might have nicked it. She was pleased as punch with that bloody thing."

"I'm glad. The place is just so dark."

"Ugh, I know. I'd quite like to move her out of there, but it's her home. I'm just not sure it's the healthiest place for her to be living."

"I guess she has her friends around the wharf and in Kings Cross."

"Yeah… I suppose you could say that. There are some very decent friends in the community. Then there are others…" May paused. "So what can I do for you Tallie?"

"I can't seem to find your mum."

"No, she's been out of town for a few months."

"Oh. Is she ok?"

"I presume so. She's on walkabout. I think she went north. Our people are from here, but mum was actually born up around Moree. Did you know that?"

"I think she mentioned it, but the place names didn't mean a lot to me."

"No, I suppose they wouldn't."

"Do you have any means of contacting her? It's nothing urgent, but we just haven't seen each other for a while."

"Mum can be hard to find sometimes. It's nice of you to check in on her."

"I've become very fond of her. She's such an interesting woman."

"She's had a hard life, but she's a good person underneath it all. She was separated from her parents by the government as a kid. They didn't think black people could raise their children right. So she was brought up by some real nasty Christian folk instead. They're the ones who put a lot of that god shit into her. She's lost now between the old dreams and the new. Can't decide if she's of Country or with Jesus."

Tallie thought about that. It fit the bill of the woman she understood. "Can I ask what it is that you believe?"

"Hmm…" May seemed to consider, "I don't believe either really. But I've tried to connect to my people and my land. Our language is lost, did you know that? The local language around Sydney. We have some words, but the rest was taken and destroyed."

"I had a loose idea."

"You're American?"

"Yeah…" Tallie felt compelled to be open. "My dad was from Louisiana, but I didn't really know him. My mom was Californian. She grew up in a cult or a commune, or some hippy bullshit. Sounds kind of similar to how Charlotte came up now that I think about it. Just a different cult. My mom somehow ended up in the Dakotas. Landed in a town where methamphetamine and guns were the two pastimes. I guess she got trapped in that time by her decisions. And by me."

"She took care of you?"

"She did. For what it was worth. For what she was capable of. She walked out when I was fifteen. Haven't heard from her since. She lacked a maternal instinct. It's a trait I share I think."

"Hmm. Sounds fucked up."

Tallie laughed. "Yeah, pretty much. I think I turned out fine in the end though."

"Well you developed good taste in lamps."

"Are you worried about your mom?"

"Nah. She's always gone on walkabout. It's been a few years, but she'll be off on some adventure. Probably good to have a break from some of those *friends* of hers. I think she likes to let her legs put a bit of distance between herself and her past sometimes. But she's getting old now. She's closer to the dreaming. Yesterday and tomorrow are the same for her. It's all on the same line. It's probably a bit hard for you to fathom, but if you walk with mum, and you ask her when you'll get there, she'll tell you at sunset, and you'll get there at sunset, but it might be that day, or the next, or a week from then. Or six months… But it will be at sunset. When you arrive."

"I see."

"She'll find you. If you need her."

19.

Tallie woke up in an unfamiliar bed in luxurious sheets. The room was clad in pale timbers, and the light filtered softly through a rice paper screen. Her mouth was dry and her head was split in two.

She remembered back a few hours. Flying in to Tokyo from Sydney. Her and Yuko at a karaoke bar with three American sailors and a backpacker from New Zealand.

The hangover was too bad to feel embarrassed about any particular bad piece of behavior, though there had been a few.

She had the vaguest memory of her and Yuko abandoning ship and escaping in a black taxi.

There was a bottle of San Pelegrino beside the bed along with a toothbrush and a towel. No amount of drunken disarray would ever stop Yuko Matsumoto from being the perfect host.

Tallie sipped greedily on the water and wondered where her phone had ended up. She looked on the other side of the bed and found that it had been attached to a charger and plugged into the wall.

Tallie checked her emails and discovered that Yuko had been awake for at least an hour. She had forwarded Tallie an email entitled: **Patsy's Lineweaver - Wow. - Fwd. Requested Analysis**. She opened the attached document.

It was an incredibly impressive interrogation of the contributing options and holdings that made up the patsy's antecedents: of their trading potential, of the surrounding threads, the short and long knots, and of the leverage that was available.

Combined with the new threads, these options weren't just good, they were better than anything else that Tallie had in hand.

They transformed The Napalm Trade from being one of very good value to being one of exceptional, perhaps extraordinary value.

She felt her excitement rising palpably, even through her hangover.

The analysis was two pages. Most lineweavers she had worked with would have achieved a fifth as much in twenty pages.

Tallie read her favorite parts again. Then she went and made a coffee and sat by the window above Yuko's garden, looking out onto a green and rust patchwork of stunted little trees. She read the analysis again from top to bottom, locking every detail into her mind.

She sat with her coffee. *Impossible*, Tallie thought to herself. This analysis was too good. Yet while it was clear to Tallie that the lineweaver was aware of the trade they were trying to make, the lineweaver was omitting just enough connecting details so that the patsy would only see that they owned a diamond, rather than an entire alluvial deposit.

This was standard practice in The House for trading with outsiders and for any externally-facing document. Tallie felt certain that this was the work of a lineweaver trained by The House.

Though when she reflected on it, it was also clear to Tallie that The Napalm Trade wasn't fully understood by this analyst. There was guesswork and supposition. They had missed several key aspects that Tallie and her team were pursuing.

But there were also three points that none of Tallie's team had come close to considering. Who the fuck was this lineweaver?

The Past Trader

She went to forward the document to Shintaro, but scrolled down to read the email copy first. The patsy had written:

> *Analysis attached. I was given permission to send it to you, but if you want to know more you're going to need to speak to the woman in Lahore.*
> *You can text her at +132320264431*
> *She advises discretion.*

Tallie paused in forwarding the email to Shintaro. She needed to know who and what she was dealing with.

Tallie wondered where Yuko was - she had been too distracted by the analysis to have given it any thought to now. Yuko had already seen the email so there was no point in trying to keep it from her. Tallie briefly wondered whether she would have hidden it otherwise.

She tuned her ears into a clinking noise from the garden. Yuko was out there. Tallie watched for a few moments and saw Yuko as she appeared from behind a zen obelisk of raw black shale, her face concealed beneath a wide-brimmed bamboo hat.

Tallie watched as the woman dropped down to her knees, and with a trowel dug a small shallow hole like a little grave. Yuko then reached beside her and lifted up a tiny delicate Bonzai, she disgorged it from its fragile blue dish and planted it roughly into the naked earth.

20.

He woke up in an insipid light. A meek dawn crept through the frail lace curtains.

He was in the apartment that Anya was billeted in. He could see the outline of the apartment block next door through the curtain. That building was still intact, but he knew that if he walked to the window there would be a scene of carnage in the surrounding neighborhood. Concrete smashed and fractured by sky-falling Russian ordinance.

But here he could close his eyes again and drift back into a half sleep and think that he was just on a holiday in the Ukrainian countryside. That he had met a girl. In a bar. And now maybe he could take her somewhere and marry her.

Anya shifted a little against him and his eyes opened again. He could see the top of her head nestled into his shoulder, which was numb, so he moved it now with that awareness.

Her hair was greasy. A dye job had stretched out to the tips. She was months from a salon. He envisioned her at one. Her natural habitat. She was born for a glamorous life. Not for this. He would kill for her to return to that exalted empty existence.

She was snoring softly. A slightly rasping sound that suggested that her sinuses weren't perfectly intact. Nothing was perfectly intact anymore.

She had relented to be his lover on the second day of his training, and on the first day she had given him a kiss.

It was a bonding of convenience and desperation. A surrender to the circumstances and a middle finger and fuck you to the same.

He thought back in time to the warriors on the steppe or in their longboats. To the Roman legions putting sword and flame into Germanic housewives. And of Syrian widows. To the coupling form that was as old as time. He felt a vicious anger towards the Russians who he knew now would threaten his dreams and his nightmares with her rape.

He had seen the aftermath of such events. And each time had felt a unique fury. Aroused, confused, horrified. Engorged with rage and impotence. A primal recognition that terrified him more than anything else that he had ever brought back from a battlefield.

He had at least taught her how to shoot straight. How to clear a stoppage.

She wasn't bad in a scrap. She had a kind of nimble viciousness. Quick to the draw and slow to ease on the trigger.

But she would never be an operator. This war was just personal.

He adjusted his arm some more because it began hurting too much.

Without opening her eyes she shifted her body and kissed him blindly on the chin. He kissed her back, and she stirred slightly into wakefulness.

"I don't want you to leave today." She said.

"I don't want to leave either."

"But you're going to leave aren't you?"

"Of course I'm going to leave."

"But we'll see each other again?"

"Yes."

He didn't believe it. He believed the opposite if he was honest with himself.

She shifted herself and opened her eyes to look at him skeptically. They both knew it was a lie. But then they both were certain of nothing and uncertain of everything.

She smiled as though she shared that realization in that moment. "Well, hopefully I'll see you again soon."

"Hopefully... I really do hope so." He corrected himself.

She nodded. "Well I have your fucking number. It's not like we're in the stone age. Not yet."

"No, not yet."

"If you kill a man, even if you do it viciously, I want you to feel better about it because you're doing it for me."

He laughed. "And if you kill a woman. I want you to feel better about it. Because you're doing it for me. Because I'd hate to have to choose between her and you."

She rolled her eyes and lay back on his shoulder. "Do you think I could kill a man or a woman?"

"I'm sure of it."

"Good. Then you did your job."

They lay in silence for a while.

"When I was 17," she told him, "I would dance with Russians and we would take ecstasy tablets and swim together in the sea. The water would surround your body and the whole world would feel at one and safe and connected."

"It sounds nice."

"I don't understand how we got from there to here."

He lifted his head and looked across the room at the two rifles that were leant against the wall. "I think that our civilization is really, really bad at choosing tools."

21.

The immigration hall in Lahore was hustle and chaos. A Pakistani man approached her immediately, one of several in drab suits wearing lanyards. He looked official, but this wasn't her first rodeo.

He reached for her documents. "Come, I will take you through the queue."

"How much?" Tallie asked suspiciously, clutching her documents and her passport.

"Two thousand rupees, very good price."

"Two hundred."

The man looked horrified. "No, no. That's too little. Too little." He made a show of walking away, then pretended to change his mind. "One thousand."

"Five hundred. It's my last offer. All the way to baggage."

The man frowned, but nodded sharply and took her immigration forms from her, then led her straight to the front of the queue. He put words in the ear of a border official, who glanced up at her with disinterest then waved her forward, scanned her documents briefly, stamped her passport with a sequence of aggressive thumps then let her through.

The fixer led her all the way to baggage. He was seemingly disgruntled by her knowledge of local market prices and didn't attempt any conversation which was a relief.

Tallie was fairly certain the correct price was closer to three hundred rupees, so she didn't feel guilty about it. She tipped one hundred rupees - about fifty cents.

Her hotel had a driver waiting for her in the arrivals hall who led her out to a small bus. She climbed aboard as the only passenger for the thirty minute ride to the hotel.

Lahore has the worst air pollution in the world - a thick gray soup of smog. Her hotel was called the Avari and stood on a garden-hemmed street near the natural history museum. All the plants and trees concealed in the haze made her feel as though she were arriving at a jungle palace emerging through the hot mist.

Security was serious and the bus was checked for bombs in a staging area before rolling on to the hotel proper.

The doormen wore slightly comical military-style outfits with ostentatious plumage on their hats like roosters on parade.

She checked in to her suite then had a shower. Once she had freshened up, she texted: [Where?]

An address came in reply. She found it on the map on her phone. It was inside the old walled city. She didn't have her bearings yet, but she noted that the address was reasonably close to the central mosque.

She felt it wise not to take a vehicle directly to the meeting in case anyone was following her. She wondered if she should turn her phone off, but that seemed pointless now that she had been messaged with a specific address.

The desk of the hotel organized for a car to drop her at the mosque.

The roads into the old city were a study in pandemonium. All types of wheeled and legged traffic scrabbling over narrow dirt roads that were barely a single car wide in places. Rich smells of roadside eats and rancid smells of open sewers seeped through the car windows. Horns and squawks and chatter. Her driver kept casting an eye back at her in the rear view mirror. She didn't feel in any real danger here, but she reflected that it would feel nice to bring the driver with her, but she had to attend this meeting solo.

The mosque was the heart of the city and an incredibly impressive building, she brought up Wikipedia on her phone and learnt that it had been built by a Mughal Emperor in 1673, just a few decades after the Taj Mahal and was significantly larger than it. It had been the biggest mosque in the world for over 300 years.

She was dropped near its entrance and had to shoo away her driver who was eager to stick around for a longer payday.

Where the Taj Mahal is white, the Badshahi mosque in Lahore is red, but their shapes are similar: onion domes and high red minarets that soar above the city, with traceries of vines and gardens adorning the internal surfaces, entangled into geometric projections of stunning complexity and symmetry. A fortress of poetic faith, and by the sheer monumentality of its scale one of the most remarkable structures Tallie had ever seen.

She took off her walking boots at the entrance and took a lap inside the mosque. The humidity was stifling and the stone floor felt hot like a furnace under her bare feet.

The Pakistanis seemed less rigid in the expression of their faith than the muslims of the Gulf on her initial impressions. Islam was evidently important here - there was no doubt of that - but these were an ancient people in an ancient city. There were other traditions and heritages with roots that ran even deeper. She noted that there were very few people praying. But a great many were gathered there in the central courtyard chatting together in groups - many of both men and women.

After a brief ten minute wander she regathered her boots then left the mosque and cut through the surrounding markets, crossing the road that she had noted from her map, then down into the rabbit warren of narrow streets. Legions of motorbikes squeezed along the mud roads, battling against people on foot, hawkers pulling barrows, donkeys, carts, and horses.

It was only the haphazard power lines, tangled in infinitudes, and the competing cacophony of motor drones and horns that guaranteed to her that the present persisted.

She tried to navigate from memory, but the streets were so slender and confusing that she had to check her bearings. She was initially concerned by the risk of flashing an expensive phone to look at the map - she was a woman on her own in what was clearly a very poor part of the city, but while she attracted a lot of eyes there was far too much disorder and she walked too quickly to gather much notice. She had wrapped her head in a green silk scarf, and wore thick black sunglasses. She had dressed down into a denim jacket, white t-shirt, and black jeans.

She was surprised to see heroin addicts along a wall, lying in the mud. Spectacular food smells burst the air as hawkers cooked curries and naan in large round pans, while the smell of human feces launched regular belligerent skirmishes across her senses.

She felt herself crawling back along the wake of the present into the past, the density and concentration of now attenuating far further than she had ever seen it. She felt transported to a present that was thousands of years earlier. To a time of filth and beasts of burden.

The Past Trader

She at last made her way to an ancient little street, overhung by four story houses with rendered ground floors, topped by precariously towering layers of ornately carved timber.

She found a turquoise gate and knocked three times. A one eyed man answered. "Welcome. You are expected."

She entered from the street and the gate was closed behind her. She had walked into an oasis of calm. A tall fountain of many colored tiles bubbled in the center of a large courtyard. Multiple doors entered a grand and elegant house.

"Please have a seat." The man suggested. "Would you like tea?"

"Yes, thank you."

She sat down on a shaded bench that faced the fountain. She could see into parts of the house. Walls painted in rich greens and maroons. Elaborate venetian chandeliers and a cavalcade of paintings. She couldn't see all of them closely, but there were colliding styles. Colonial art, Mughal art, modern photographic portraits in black and white, and even what looked like a grand 19th century impressionist work.

"Welcome to my ancestral home."

The voice was beautiful. A woman's: lyrical and musical, but polished and crisp. At once exotic and aristocratic.

Tallie turned. The woman was perhaps 50, or much older maybe, and dressed very beautifully. In silk fabrics that were arrayed in a style that was both traditional and contemporary. In shimmering golds and regal blues.

"I am Shazia. Miss Dandieu I presume?"

They shook hands. "It's nice to meet you. Call me Tallie."

"Please, come into the drawing room Tallie. The air will be cleaner."

They walked into the largest room on the ground floor. An imposing portrait of an imperious gentleman dominated the space in a gilt frame. He carried a jeweled sword and had an elaborate, almost comical mustache.

"My great grandfather." Shazia explained simply, following the focus of Tallie's attention. "He was a general but a very bad soldier. He was the instigator of two battles, both of which he lost, but he was useful to the British, so they let him keep several of his freedoms and a few of his titles, as well as some lesser indulgences, including this house."

"How generous of them."

"Quite. This was once the most cosmopolitan street in all of Lahore, though it seems hard to believe that now. My family have lived here for seven centuries."

"Wow."

"We have proved adept at navigating the political treacheries of various powers across the subcontinent. Everyone from the Mongols to the Mughals to the Jagat Seth to the Maharajas to the British. And now we survive even you and your colleagues at The House." She gave a coy smile.

"Our titles were variously revoked and returned." She continued, "Yet somehow we persisted over the eons. But I never had children and I regret that I am the very last of… *the line*." She rolled her eyes apologetically. "So as you might imagine, my one-time profession is not without irony."

"I never heard of you as a lineweaver of The House." Tallie admitted.

The Past Trader

"No? Really? Well, I would feel insulted, but there are of course several parties who would quite like for me to be forgotten. Though as I'm sure you deduced from my capacity to have found you in the first place, I am not entirely left without friends. Thus it was I who was able to provide you with your..." She paused theatrically as though remembering the word, "Patsy!"

"Yes, you have certainly demonstrated your reach." Tallie acknowledged, "And your very considerable talents. It was probably the best analysis I've ever seen."

Shazia tilted her head in a slight bow.

"So why did you leave The House?" Tallie asked.

"Nobody leaves The House." She said shortly. "But in any event, I am... *semi* retired. I was put out to pasture more or less. Some of my views were seen as -" she waved an arm, "- competitive."

"Competitive with whom?" Tallie asked.

"With the orthodoxy. I came to wonder whether any of our strategies truly work. The evidence isn't as strong as you think. Of course we make profit, but there could be various explanations for that. Changing the past is not the sort of solution that Occam would have deduced with his razor I assure you. And conservation of energy becomes rather awkward."

"You must have seen the impact of severed threads?" Tallie said skeptically.

The woman shrugged. "I might have seen many things."

Tallie raised an eyebrow. "So if you didn't think any of it was real, why would you still be weaving lines?"

Shazia laughed. "Girl's got to make a living." She lifted her hand to summon the man with one eye who had stopped at the door. He entered the room and served the tea. The women sat down across from each other on slightly moth-eaten embroidered silk couches: Tallie's in blue, Shazia's in green.

"Thank you Sulman."

He bowed.

"Sulman has helped me for a long time. His old age and feigned obsolescence do not entirely conceal significant capabilities. He lost that eye in a skirmish at the Khyber Pass. He cut out the other man's throat. He's a dangerous adversary. Do you have many adversaries Miss Dandieu?"

"I have none of note."

"I find that hard to believe." She sipped her tea and regarded Tallie clinically. "You have a wonderful reputation in the firm. You are seen as ruthless. Even by the standards of The House."

"I do my job to the best of my abilities."

"Oh you do more than that." She put her tea down on the table. "You are no doubt puzzled by why I asked you here?"

"The thought did cross my mind."

"I knew that curiosity was one of your finest features. I appealed to the best in you, not the worst. I feel that's the ideal way to start a friendship."

"So you say. But you haven't appealed for anything yet, other than asking me to travel so far to visit you. What is it that you want Shazia?"

"Do not make this trade."

"Do not make it?" Tallie asked in disbelief. "Why would you have sent me the patsy?"

"Other reasons… To test you."

The Past Trader

Tallie scowled then slowly put down her tea. "So, to surmise events: you learned - somehow - of a trade that I am making. You put the pieces together and found me the keystone for the entire enterprise. You provided analysis to that crucial piece, thereby guaranteeing their participation. You enacted multiple layers of obscurity and secrecy to bring yourself to my attention. You had me cross the world to Pakistan on the auspices of providing additional information that will guarantee the trade. And yet now - you tell me not to play?"

"Well put like that my actions seem awfully theatrical don't they?"

"They do."

"What do you understand of the religion of this place? You saw the mosque earlier I believe?"

Tallie frowned at the woman's knowledge of her movements: this gave her a good idea of how Fred had found her at LAX - perhaps the one eyed man. Though in the back of her mind she conceded that the mosque was pretty hard to miss if you were coming into this part of town.

"I'm largely ignorant of Islam," Tallie answered after a moment, "I tried reading the Koran once. I found it tough going."

"Come, let me show you something." Shazia led Tallie up a beautifully carved timber stair. Upstairs was another room bursting with ornamentation and artifact - like an entire season of *Antiques Roadshow* squeezed between four walls.

They crossed through this room into another filled with statues carved in gray or black granites, and embedded with impossibly fine quartzes that glittered under the sapphire murano chandelier.

It all looked incredibly ancient. Eight statues lined the far wall. Five busts and three full-length figures in varying degrees of repair, some almost perfect.

The statues were seemingly Buddhist. But the style was more... muscular than Tallie had seen before. Rippling chests and stone halos.

"Have you heard of Gandhara?" Shazia quizzed.

"No." Tallie acknowledged.

"It was a Buddhist culture. A dominant force in these parts for over 800 years. Part of a quasi-Greek civilization that followed after Alexander. These are Gandharan princes. Bodhisattvas. Saints I suppose. Ones who spent incalculable eons reaching enlightenment, then upon finding it, cast themselves back upon the wheel."

She gestured up at the most immaculate of the statues. A towering gray Buddhist prince perhaps eight feet tall, perfect but for missing hands, draped in Roman-style robes. The face was distinctly asiatic. Buddha-like features and a curling top knot beset with jewels carved into the stone. The artistry was magnificent - the muscular physique perfectly proportioned. Even the necklaces and sandals were chiseled in precise and immaculate detail.

"Did you know that Alexander the Great came all this way?"

"I've read as much." Tallie answered. "But don't know the details."

"Alexander the Great was one of the worst tyrants and most vicious psychopaths that ever strode this earth. Yet with the sword he brought cultural magnificence. And shoots of renewal crawled up in his wake across the scorched and salted earth. Would you forgive him his trespasses?"

"No." Tallie answered simply.

"Nor I." Shazia agreed.

"But what would you say of one who does not add the salt in the first place, but who has the means to modify the density of that salt after the fact, and adjust the duration by which it stains the earth?"

Tallie didn't like where this was going. "Your equivalence is a simplification of the abstract."

"Oh, I like that." Shazia smiled lazily. She turned back to the statue: "The art of Gandhara was especially strong in the second and third centuries of the common era when the Greek influence was strongest. Then again later in the fourth. It was of course individual artists who provided that prodigiousness, though their names are forgotten to time."

Shazia led Tallie to the opposite wall. There were more Buddhas here crammed onto a teak table amongst other statues, but they were no longer carved from stone, but molded from clay, and even from bronze. But far smaller, and mostly much cruder. "By the fifth century the work was usually built out of this -" she carefully picked up a Buddha head, "- Stucco. Plaster. Dust. And the greatest artists and their techniques were becoming disconnected from their line. Though the Gandharans still carved in stone sometimes. But on a tremendous scale!"

She turned to Tallie and her eyes glittered in the light. "Towering statues of the Buddha, more than ten stories high! The Taliban detonated them in the '90s. In Afghanistan. Do you remember that?"

"Yes." Tallie remembered vaguely.

"Hewn from stone, but rendered in plaster. They fell easily enough. In the end."

Shazia put down the Buddha's head and ran her fingers across another little sculpture - of a young boy with flowing hair, made from an orange terracotta-like stucco. "From hard granite, to less eternal clay, to residue of gunpowder. That is the arc that time enabled for those monuments that celebrated the first great one to have broken the wheel of time."

"In this instance." Tallie said.

"Yes… in this instance." Shazia regarded her shrewdly. "Come. We should finish our tea."

They crossed back through the other room. Shazia waved her hand vaguely at all the cluttered objects, "Each of these works will tell you a history. A mangling of unwoven lines."

Tallie followed the woman across the room, but paused midway down the stairs, her eye caught by a tiny painting of a Mughal king, so immaculately detailed that it was almost indistinguishable from a photo - save for all the minute elements in real gold.

"That is a portrait of Ali Khan Bahadur, the Nawab of Rampur. It is painted on ivory. The artist used one single hair to create it. A tiny imperceptible brush. It took them 15 years." She paused a moment in reverie as she peered across at the phone-sized object. She turned sharply to Tallie: "Do you really think a mere mass of capital can easily disassemble such patience?"

Tallie regarded the woman without emotion. "Quite the opposite. I would define such patience as an extremely large block of capital. It is that capital which has ensured its passage in time."

The Past Trader

Tallie folded her arms. "I really do not understand why you have taken the path that you have. You are filled with contradictions. You claim our profession false, yet you led me here under the auspices that my actions are essential."

Shazia smiled. "Have you ever really run the numbers on how often The House gets it right Tallie? Yes we make profit, but our record is spotty at best. Bad investments will haunt you for much longer than you realize. Perhaps I perceive the weight of regret more clearly than you Tallie, maybe that is all. Perhaps I wish to protect you from impending and very long-lasting, deep woven regret."

"And why would you have any interest in protecting me? You've never met me until today. If anyone is regretting their decisions here, it is clearly you. You gave birth to a part of this trade, and now you seek to undo it -"

"Be more subtle in your thinking Tallie." Shazia chided her. "You disappoint me."

"...You want me to break the trade. Wipe out Tatsuma."

"Close. And that would be nice. And indeed -" Shazia put a finger to her chin, "- that might be an outcome necessitated by the events that I counsel..." she nodded slowly as though thinking about it for the first time. "But no, I don't much like Tatsuma, but I do not despise him either. I do not *trust* him, but his interest is naked and I do not fear the self-regard of others if I have no reliance upon it. I just pity it somewhat. There is a far bigger trade to make. Don't you see?"

"Show me."

22.

Tallie flew to San Francisco. The homelessness seemed to have doubled since she had last been here, though it had already seemed unimaginable. Wild meandering queues of destitution - of filth and unchecked mental illness. Waiting in ill-defined lines for nothing. For the time that was already lost to them. Queues to the void.

She regretted her choice of staying in the city but knew that she wouldn't be here for long. She dropped her bags at the hotel, showered, and ordered a car to take her straight to Silicon Valley. She worked from the back seat on her way there.

The patsy lived in a typically boring house in Palo Alto. Tallie had visualized it before she arrived and her expectations were completely on point: a tastefully done showhome that had been bought rather than thought about, and occupied rather than lived in.

She was buzzed into a courtyard populated by a Porsche, with sweeping glass windows that revealed expensive art, mostly of bad taste - Alec Monopoly and vintage Star Wars posters.

The patsy opened the front door in a Versace shirt with too many buttons undone, exposing his slightly pigeoned chest. He had the self-satisfied look of an aspirational playboy who has trapped a damsel in his fuck palace. Tallie's expression stopped him in his tracks.

He swallowed. "Nice to see you again."

He led her through to the open plan living area. "Champagne?" He suggested, "- or... or coffee?"

"Coffee's fine."

He began to fiddle with a fancy cappuccino machine.

"So I understand that Yuko has sketched out the options for you?" She asked.

"That's right."

"But you have some misgivings?"

He turned and gave a weak smile. "A few."

"The '50s General Motors trades have the highest value you're transacting. Their current market price is 60% of your antecedents. Now the other approach - that your mysterious lineweaver proposed - is to juice more aggressively in the '70s. That would provide more dynamic leverage in your mother's employment history."

"What about my father's timeline?"

"That's more difficult. As a merchant sailor he was very close to a lot of large industries. Shipping during the oil crisis was problematic. There's an enormous amount of capital embedded in the status quo. Did you read what Yuko sent you about trading against entropic flows?"

"I tried to."

"It can be done." Tallie said firmly, "But you need a lot of capital and you get a lot of chaotic turbulence. With the amount of capital that we're deploying our margin of safety gets eaten to shit."

"Ok." He said, "So we focus on my mother."

"It's our best prospect for an optimal outcome... for you." She opened her briefcase.

She withdrew the documents and put them in front of him. The man flipped through them idly: weighted decision trees, woven timelines.

The Past Trader

Tallie really wasn't sure why on earth the man was doing this. The potential benefit wasn't guaranteed, and the downside could be spectacular. She was sure that he was smart enough to see that.

She wondered if he was having second thoughts. Whether he perhaps felt compelled because so many people had been working on this - locked into his choice by the actions of others and the sequence of events that seemed most obvious to him.

"What do you think the most likely outcome is?" He asked.

"Of this proposed strategy? 2x return. 10x cash return on your initial investment. You made it 12 years ago, so that's almost 22% compound. Far better than you would have done in most other financial assets."

He grunted and nodded. "Yeah. Ok… Yeah."

"You want to lock in the trade?"

He looked at her. The bravado was gone. There was a child-like quality. A naivety that stirred Tallie slightly, but not enough to move her.

"I think this is a good strategy." He said. As if he were talking himself into believing it.

"I do too." *Good for whom*, she wondered.

"Let's pull the trigger."

*   *   *

The patsy walked Tallie out to her car. He was asking a lot of questions that he should have asked half an hour ago before he signed.

"We've also booby trapped a few lines to protect your main trade." She explained to him. "That's where that excess capital has gone."

"You booby trap lines?" He asked in amazement. "How do you booby trap lines?"

She looked at him and wondered whether this was detail that she should disclose. "It's one of the ways you hedge a past. Essentially you take something like a short position on a line that could block your trade. If all goes normal on your main transaction then you'll wipe out a couple of million or billion bucks depending on how big the hedge was. But if someone tries to be clever and attack your main position you can squeeze them hard enough to make them bleed out of their eyeballs. You poison the surrounding lines basically. Salt the earth."

"Fuck. Does that happen often?"

"No. But it's funny when it does."

She watched his reaction. He nodded slowly.

She climbed into her limousine and waved goodbye.

23.

There was a clunking sound as the javelin missile leapt from the tube propped on Alexi's shoulder and traveled almost lazily for its first 20 meters, then its main rocket engine ignited and it tore up into the sky with a primal scream.

Jimmy's binoculars were still on the target, his elbows wedged into the grass, and he put his eyes back on it, blinking away the missile's incandescent streak. He was 40 meters to the left and 20 behind the two man fireteam of Oleg and Alexi. He could just see the Russian tank framed between the ridges of two hills. He couldn't quite tell from this distance, but it looked like the tank might be a T90, one of the newer ones.

The missile was screeching up high to rain death down on to this angular box of war, and eviscerate its occupants with vicious kinetic and thermal energy and a spray of molten copper. The binoculars shook in Jimmy's hands from the adrenaline. The time stretched out into a singular long, straining, attenuated moment...

He saw the missile hit in a brilliant flash that evolved into a large fireball. Smoke followed immediately in its wake. After a time they heard the blast - a single deep drum beat that trailed off to a grumble.

It looked like a kill. Cheers and ecstatic Ukrainian curses went up from around the edges of the woods.

"This is sugar one. Strike on target. Over." Jimmy radioed.

Oleg was sprinting back to cover. Alexi was lazily disassembling the tube. *Don't do that*, Jimmy thought as he stood up to yell at him, but then Alexi vanished in an instantaneous eruption of earth and fire.

Jimmy picked himself up in a haze and spat metallic dirt out of his mouth, then began yelling at his team. "Fall back you cunts!"

What the fuck was that? Jimmy wondered. These fuckers were dialled in. He was so confused by the blast that he wasn't sure if it was counter-artillery or another tank.

Something obviously had a pretty good idea of where the javelin had come from.

Shells began saturating the area. Two more strikes landed with sharp cracking booms - artillery - blessedly in the opposite direction to where most of his team were. Shrapnel whistled past. He paused and looked back at where Alexi had been. He knew the survival chance was zero. *Fuck, fuck, fuck.*

"This is coffee one. Movement on the road." Greco's voice came through his earpiece. The man sounded cool as a cucumber. "Four vehicles. Two AFVs. One car. One tank. Booking it southwards."

Fuck Jimmy thought. That was fast.

"Coffee will engage in one klick. Over." Greco continued.

"Was that first strike a tank or artillery?" Jimmy asked over the radio.

"Artillery. Stand by. Over."

Fuck.

For the return fire to have been that quick it meant that it was probably an A.I. targeting them, and not some poorly-paid, worse-motivated Russian.

This meant that their ability to use anti-tank systems was going to be compromised. They had another three javelin set up to ambush the armored counter-attack that they were expecting, but only one of the systems was unmanned. Those other two fireteams were going to be heavily exposed.

It was El Greco's call, but Jimmy was thinking about what he would be doing. *Pull one team back, sacrifice the other.* They needed to make a dent on at least two more pieces of armor to slow them down. One more strike on its own would probably not be enough.

Jimmy hustled his unit back into the woods for more cover. There was white fear on the surrounding faces, but they were all professionals here. Grieving for Alexi would come later.

"Sugar. This is coffee one. Reposition to midtown. I repeat, reposition to midtown. Over." Greco called the play.

"Coffee one. This is sugar one. Midtown confirmed. Over." Jimmy acknowledged.

Fuck. His team kept moving back behind the tree line. Greco's order told Jimmy that the Russian armor was choosing to cut across the field rather than follow the road all the way down to the bend. Jimmy's unit were being moved to box in the less optimal ambush point. This meant Greco's fire teams were going to need to engage sooner rather than later. This meant that everything wasn't quite going to the plan they had hoped for.

Sure enough, Jimmy soon heard a distant clunk and whoosh as another Javelin engaged. Again the counter-artillery followed quickly - almost instantaneously this time. Flashes of firepower. In the ensuing orgy of noise and chaos Jimmy lost the capacity to second guess what was happening. His team hustled forward, running along a wooded slope.

"This is coffee one. We have another three strikes on targets. Over." Greco updated calmly.

Jimmy felt his guts move. Jesús was angry - El Greco had sacrificed both his fireteams. In his heart Jimmy knew that Greco had made the right play - if they didn't give the impression that they were a larger force than they were, the Russians might counterattack with too much confidence and kill the lot of them. Even losing another four guys now was probably better for the overall survivability of the unit.

It was a fucking death metal calculus.

"Coffee repositioning." Greco radioed, "Tea has the play. Over."

"Confirmed. Tea is downtown. Over." The Canadian replied - he was up on the far hill guarding their flank. He and his two man team would have a better view of the coming carnage. Their role was to stay hidden and call in support.

Jimmy's team moved efficiently through the forest towards their next fire position closer to the crest of the eastern hill. His eyes kept scanning upwards for drones.

They couldn't see any movement on the visible section of road when they got there. The Russian artillery had swept over them to the west, and now they could hear rolling blasts of heavy calibers in the distance. The big Ukranian guns were talking back, and were likely closer than the Russians had expected.

Greco and his surviving guys came in from the other side of the hill. It looked like they were missing two. Greco was propping a casualty between his and one of the Ukranian's shoulders. He seemed to take a visual tally of Jimmy's guys. "Sugar two?" He asked Jimmy as he lowered the wounded man.

Alexi. Jimmy shook his head.

"This is coffee one. Coffee and sugar reunited, over." Greco radioed the Canadian.

"Roger that coffee one. Over."

Greco and his medic began to do a repair job on Len - the injured soldier. His left leg looked fucked up. He would probably lose it. Below the ankle if he was lucky. They had tourniquet'd the fuck out of it, and Greco was now dressing it in his own inflation cuff. Jimmy was pretty confident it would be the only inflation cuff Greco had brought along for this trip. The boy Len was letting out a sustained choking moan. He was going to be a bitch for them to casevac.

It wasn't easy letting your men die. It was a decision Jimmy had only imagined until recently. Now he had made that call twice.

Three of them were already deleted on this particular trip beyond the wire. It was the worst casualty count Jimmy had ever been a part of, but then it looked like they might have swatted as many as three or even four armored vehicles. Command would see this as a success. Even if none of them made it back from here this would still look like a success.

Jimmy checked his watch. "Two mikes." He said to Greco, warning him they needed to move. The man nodded but didn't look up from the trauma care on Len. The other guys were chewing down chocolate or water. Things could get uglier quick, and the counterattack was sure to come.

The distant artillery duel was picking up pace. It sounded like more guns had joined the fight.

They lifted Len on a roll-up stretcher and hustled through the woods towards the southern end of the tree line. With two carrying the wounded and subtracting the Canadian's team that left eleven fighting men ready for instant engagement. Eleven down from twenty.

Jimmy's group fanned out in the vanguard. Moving a little slower than they would like so that the casualty could be brought up the middle.

"Contact." The Canadian radioed.

Fuck.

"Infantry patrol... looks -" The Canadian cut off and they heard small arms fire in the distance. Over the hill, but seemingly coming out of the same part of the woods that they were in.

This was a bad outcome.

A searing bright light smashed Jimmy off his feet and pancaked the air out of his chest. *Boom, boom, boom, boom, boom, boom, boom.*

He felt the earth rattle beneath him. He scrunched his eyes closed amidst the heat and the dirt.

His ears were blocked but eventually the world returned to stillness. He waited a moment then crawled up on to his hands and knees and grasped his rifle and shook away the soil. *"What the fuck was thaaaaat -"* he slurred.

Greco was going ballistic. It took a few seconds for the words to make sense: "Smerch, smerch!"

Smerch rockets. *Fuck.* Someone was calling heavy duty guns on to their position. They drew away from the rockets blindly, back into the denser part of the trees, the woods behind them were burning and the air reeked. Jimmy started to get his shit together. He maneuvered his guys into slightly better defensive positions. He could taste blood and it occurred to him that he should check himself for injury. He was bleeding from the forehead, but it didn't seem too bad. Two more of Greco's soldiers were injured but could still fight.

"Tea one. Where the fuck are they? Over." Jimmy radioed.

"Guns are out of range." Came the Canadian, his breathing heavy, "Infantry is to the south east of downtown. Twenty strong. I repeat, twenty infantry south east of downtown. We've disengaged and are drawing back. Over."

"Sugar one. Confirmed."

Jimmy looked across to Greco who was with their wounded further behind. He hustled over to him.

"We're going to need to flank these fuckers." Jesús told Jimmy with poison in his eyes. El Greco spread his map out in the dirt while Jimmy waved two other soldiers across to join them. The rest moved into defensive positions.

"We're going to need to get up on to this ridge line." Greco rubbed his finger along the contours.

Jimmy looked closely at the elevated terrain running up into the woods. "We're going to need to move fucking fast." He noted.

"My guys will come along here in a line." Greco traced out the next position and the movement of his central fireteam. "You guys fight up to the ridge and we'll hit their flank as we push through the middle. We'll try and maneuver them out towards the flat then the Canadian can double back and reengage them from the other side. They'll try and stay in the woods. Once they've been hit you're going to need to wheel up further to the north then push across."

Jimmy nodded. He retraced the plan twice with his own finger, visualizing the terrain. It was the best they could do in the circumstances, but at the same moment he realized this was a sacrificial play as well. And he was the bait. He didn't question it. It was just something he noted in the back of his mind. This was war.

"Good." Jimmy agreed.

They would leave their rucks here plus one man with the casualty and this would become their fall-back spot. Jimmy called over Lomidze the Georgian - probably the best remaining soldier in his group - and Jimmy recited the plan back to him with El Greco there to confirm. Lomidze tilted his head as he realized the likely consequences of this plan. He would take over when Jimmy had fallen. The man looked at Jimmy and Greco in turn then nodded.

Jimmy and Lomidze fell back to their other men and outlined the plan. "We have to take the ridge." He reiterated. "Let's move. I'll be forward scout."

Jimmy put that deadly mantle upon himself and positioned Lomidze in the rear. They hustled into the bushes as quickly as they could through the first seventy five meters, then Jimmy started moving much more cautiously. His other two guys - Oleg and Vargas the Colombian, moved along behind him in a wedge. He took out his earpiece and killed the radio so that his focus was total.

His guys knew what they were doing and let him keep at least ten meters to the front.

The Past Trader

He was dialing into the landscape. Mindful of the contours beneath the trees. The woods were as silent as a cathedral. Even the insects had shut the fuck up. His ears were ringing but they always rang. He kept his eyes out of focus so he could better detect movement, scanning left to right then back again. A rustle in the trees. A glint of light off an old piece of tin.

Jimmy stopped every few meters to reabsorb. He was moving much faster than he would if he were on a long range patrol, but they needed to get up onto that elevated ground before the enemy did. It was a pretty marginal topological advantage, but it was non-zero and should give them the best position.

If the enemy patrol knew what it was doing, it would be making for the same piece of land. So far the Russian soldiers had been a mixed bag. The Taliban understood shooting positions far better than these guys. They would have already put a machine gun up there and would be raking hell down upon them right about now.

As Jimmy got closer it was crystal clear that the Russians hadn't had the same idea. This should have made him happy, but it put him on edge because it suggested they had some other plan.

From up on the ridge there was a slight hollow visible below them with a stream passing through it. If the enemy patrol was where Jimmy thought it was, the Russians were either going to need to move around this hollow to their right and on to the ridge that Jimmy and his guys were occupying, or go to their left towards Greco. He positioned his team to ambush either direction.

"Sugar in position. Over." He radioed.

Small arms fire. A machine gun at full death rattle. A pop of a grenade. Radio silence.

Jimmy felt the fear rising in a horrible wave of anguish. A deep part of him wanted to run away. Throw down his weapons. Beg them for mercy. Let him go home. To America, to Australia, to wherever the fuck.

Jimmy peered down his rifle sight and thumbed down the safety.

A movement beyond the edge of the hollow. A shaken branch, then another.

He pulled on the trigger out of nerves and felt the reassuring firmness of a lot of graphite. The weapon didn't fire. He softened his grip and tried to control his breathing.

He saw a Russian soldier in his crosshairs. Then another.

He let them get further into the kill zone. Three soldiers. Very alert. They were looking towards the ridge line nervously. They had figured it out too late. They came closer.

Fuck, Jimmy concluded in terror. He pulled the trigger.

24.

The heat baked the turf. The usual thick green lawn of Hyde Park looked scorched and sickly. The world and the cosmos seemed to spin beneath Tallie's feet. Like she were a circus performer, balancing atop a rolling orb. Her jacket was folded over her arm and she could feel the sweat running down her flanks.

She was crossing towards Mayfair from Kensington Gardens. She had first crossed this park years before, when she was much younger. Had watched the squirrels on the bough and felt some transposition of the first home she could remember on to this place.

She felt her phone vibrate in her bag and contemplated not answering. When she looked she saw that it was a +61 Australian number.

"This is Tallie."

"Hello doll. How are you doing?" Charlotte croaked.

"Charlotte! I missed you."

"So I hear. You weren't in town for long?"

"No. A whirlwind. Just a few days. I'm in London now."

"Oh. I caught you at a bad time?"

"No. No, the opposite. How have you been?" Tallie asked.

"I'm gettin' old darlin'."

"May told me you were on walkabout."

"*Walkabout?*" Charlotte squawked, amused, "I guess you could say that. Hard to go on walkabout when there's so many roads and buildings and freeways across the land. Fences too."

"Where did you get to? Are you still away?"

Charlotte ignored the question. "We used to follow lines did you know? Songlines."

"I've heard of this."

"My people didn't have maps you see? But the song tells you about the land. All you have to do is sing it and follow its line. Follow what it says. The hills, the ridges, the rivers, even the roads. The song tells you where they are. You can walk far without losing your way. Thousands of miles if you know the song."

"It sounds ingenious."

"It isn't just an idea in our heads. It's how the land speaks to us. It's the language of the spirits that made it."

Tallie had read about these song lines and Charlotte talked about them constantly. More now than she did before.

The hours-long songs encoded a continent's worth of topology in their tone, tempo, and melody. People had crossed the entire vast Australian continent navigating by them.

"The songs tell the story of the spirits you see darl. The great snake and the sky father created the everywhen. Their songs and the songs of the animals and ancestors weave the land."

Ahead of Tallie, the snarling traffic slithered towards the Thames. Red buses, black cabs, mini cabs, hire cars, bicycles.

"I would love to understand the songs."

Charlotte laughed sharply. "You can't mate, they're sacred! We wouldn't teach you mob. I'm hoping some of my kids learn them though."

"Your daughter May is a good person." Tallie commented.

"Yup. She is."

"You must be so proud of her."

"I am. Are you alright doll? You sound a bit stressed or… different."

"I've got a weight on my shoulders." Tallie confessed. "On one side - there's an action that could make my career. On the other side I've been warned that if I do that thing that I need to, a lot of people could be affected by it. Killed maybe. Sort of. I've been asked to sabotage myself so that doesn't happen."

"Sabotage yourself? Who would have asked you to do that?"

"Someone who thinks they've done a better job of plotting out the truth of things than I have."

"Someone who knows better?" Charlotte asked.

"Yeah."

"Do you really think their judgment is that much better than yours darl?"

"I don't know. Probably."

"You're the smartest girl I ever met... How could *you* cause people to die?" Charlotte asked doubtfully, "I thought you were just a banker?"

Tallie laughed. "No, not quite."

"I don't understand much about your world, but I reckon if someone tells you they're better at predicting the future than anyone else is, you should treat what that person says as bullshit."

Tallie laughed. "What about the land? Does the land explain the future and the past?"

"The land doesn't know of those things. It's both of those things. The land sustains the ancestors, past and present. It's everything we are and will, would, or could ever be. Jesus understood what the land is. But I dunno, you probably don't

143

need to think about that stuff. Just figure out how important your career is and how much the money's worth. It seems easier if you think of it like that."

"It seems easier." Tallie laughed. "Where are you at the moment Charlotte?"

"Some wild place. But even here there's roads. And this phone works. We always live now. No matter how much we might wish we lived then." Charlotte paused for a few beats. "Anyway, I'd better get goin' darl."

"It was so nice to hear from you."

"I just wanted to check in. Heard you were looking out for me. You take care of yourself ok? Don't let anyone push you around."

"I won't."

"Lots of love darlin'."

"You too. Thanks for the call."

Tallie felt her eyes water as she hung up, possessed by the overwhelming feeling that she would never speak to Charlotte again.

She walked for an hour, through Mayfair, and all the way to St Paul's. Then she turned away south and arrived at the bridge that crossed over the river towards the Tate Modern. She peered up at the industrial strangeness of the building. A power station that had become a tomb for art.

The woman in Pakistan had proposed that more than half a million people would be eradicated by The Napalm Trade, and that twice as many again would be mutilated and burnt. That countless many would suffer in the present. That she would drag a wheel of carnage forward, through all of time.

The Past Trader

Tallie patted her pocket and found a 50 pence piece. She ran her fingers over the angles and looked down into the murky Thames. And tossed the coin.

25.

Tallie had been surprised by the restaurant that Jimmy nominated when they met in Manhattan, years earlier. He had kept a sort of loose contact with Tallie, dropping her the occasional line ever since their first "date" in Sydney: a text message from out of the blue, or a poorly formatted email every six months or so.

Jimmy seemed to think of Tallie as a sort of distant flame. A pot on the boil somewhere. In a kitchen he could only imagine and that he evidently hoped to cook at one day.

From Tallie's perspective Jimmy was damaged. Both by Marius who she loved, but mostly by war and by the trillion fractalling imperfections that had inspired him to seek out that battlefield in the first place.

His outfit that night was expensive. Dripping in designer names. It was the sort of look that marked out the nouveau riche in cities like Shanghai and Dubai, but she didn't quite understand it, because Jimmy should have had access to Marius' money. But she supposed he hadn't really grown up with it. He wore his watch in a way that dominated his wrist and that was impossible not to notice. Tallie didn't even like watches on men.

"It's nice to see you Tallie." He gave her a kiss on both cheeks.

So cosmopolitan, she thought, then checked herself and decided to not be snarky. "It's been a long time Jimmy."

"Yeah. A lot of water under a lot of bridges."

"No doubt. Did you blow any of them up?"

He smiled. "Only the one over the River Kwai."

She didn't quite know what that meant, but had a vague recollection of some cultural relevance.

"This isn't the sort of restaurant I would have expected you to suggest Jimmy." She looked around at the settings - a futurist ceiling like the white ribcage of a fallen leviathan. Enormous bundles of fresh cut cherry blossoms gathered into giant vases. Dangling lanterns like golden orbs. White leather booths. This was an opulent place even by the standards of Midtown.

"I've got my own money for the first time in my life. Why not spend it?"

"That's a dangerous attitude." She commented, and they exchanged a smile.

Jimmy was a handsome guy and she knew that the two of them would look like an interesting couple.

Tallie felt that she was clear-eyed when it came to her looks. She knew the effect she could have on men. She had been in rooms with models and actresses and knew she wasn't one of them, but in most settings she was considered attractive. The thing she liked best about working for The House was that it was the only place she had ever known where her looks meant nothing. The market simply didn't care.

Jimmy ordered a bottle of Moët and a half dozen oysters without asking Tallie whether she ate them. Or whether she wanted a drink.

"So what's been happening in the past?" Jimmy asked.

"Nothing. Signal attenuation I suppose."

"Do you want to know what I've always wondered -" Jimmy began. Tallie half paid attention as she eyeballed the other patrons. It was a certain Manhattan social set. Not the older world. This was a faster room. "- and what I've never understood about your profession?"

Tallie thought about saying something smart-assed but returned her attention and noticed the serious look on his face. "What's that Jimmy?"

"The lack of adversary."

Tallie dialed into what he had just said and couldn't quite figure it out. "What do you mean?"

"Dad always says that as a trader you're trying to beat *the market*... which is some hivemind, god-like thing. An aggregated conscious or... something."

"I guess -"

"That isn't really an adversary though is it? You're not really at war with anyone else are you?"

Tallie rubbed her lip. She thought about it. "Often you're at war with another fund. I was once told that any trade you make, your first thought should always be who's trying to fuck you on the other side of it. If you're buying they're selling. And they're selling because they think they can get an advantage over you by buying at that price."

"But you've just described a clash between two individuals." Jimmy observed, "How does the market fit into that picture?"

"Well... I guess sometimes it helps to refine the market to a singular identity. But generally speaking it's *best* to view it as an aggregated whole. Best or... most productive maybe. It sets the price."

"It's just weird to me." Jimmy continued. "In my line of work there's always an adversary. Someone who's trying to kill you, and that you're trying to kill first. It's quite clean. Sure there's political strife and freedom fighters, and all sorts of reasons why you might not want to kill that adversary, but there's an *opposition* - a conflict. I don't really understand how you live without an adversary."

Tallie looked at Jimmy thoughtfully. He is his father's son she remembered. "The market is the adversary." She tried. "But at any given point we can only really touch one or two cells of it - one or two grid squares in that vast plane of surface area. But it isn't a zero-sum game. The people we trade with - the other point of contact embodying the market in that particular trade - some days we beat them, some days they beat us. We have an ongoing trading relationship that is profitable to both of us in the long term."

"So the market isn't necessarily an adversary?"

"No. And the market isn't a zero sum game either."

"You create something from nothing?"

"I suppose."

"It's all just a big game of cooperation? Everyone getting richer?"

"Not quite." She considered. "Sometimes you get your ass kicked. Sometimes you get lucky."

"But you don't squeeze the trigger?"

"Not to kill. Not usually. Sometimes..." She was about to say more but then thought better of it.

The Past Trader

Jimmy looked at her shrewdly. "If you trade guns or weapons, and someone else uses that gun or weapon, do you think you're accountable?"

"I don't know."

"You've traded worse than guns haven't you."

"From time to time."

"So you're your own adversary?"

"That's one way of looking at it." Tallie conceded.

26.

With a trade like the Napalm Trade it wasn't as simple as Tallie pulling a trigger.

The House wasn't a corporation so much as a cartel of the best traders in the world. Each trader protected and enabled the other's positions. As lead trader on this, Tallie had already begun accumulating positions and would not provide anyone beyond her core team and Tatsuma the full details of her trade. But she would provide The House with just enough information for the collective to get a taste, and to ensure that nobody would get obliterated on any conflicting positions.

The CIOs or Chief Investment Officers were a triumvirate of the three best managers in The House. Theirs was probably the only role more complex than a lineweaver. The managers were savants. The very best traders sometimes became managers, but it was a different art. To some extent the triumvirate was an administrative position - the CIOs were the field marshalls behind the lines of battle. Prodigious traders like Marius and Tatsuma preferred to run their own books and get their hands bloody.

By forewarning The House of her trade, there was of course - in theory - a risk of some other trader optimizing for short-term opportunity and wiping out her entire book. But The House had a near immaculate record for selecting employees who shared both a long-term mentality and a disdain for naked greed. The House always wins.

Plus a trader like Tallie was smart enough to boobie trap certain trading lines. Trading against a past the size of The

Napalm Trade with incomplete data and limited warning was a recipe for obliteration.

Once a trade had been put to the triumvirate, the CIOs would factor out the spill: the impacts to the past and the future, and the tangential lines that would be snapped and rewoven in all the disparate portfolios held by The House. It wasn't just the immediate upside or downside that needed to be considered and hedged. All positions along both arrows of time were recalculated for exposure. If a portfolio was on the right side of a trade the upside could be gigantic. If they were caught flat-footed they could be annihilated. The CIOs' trading orders were always couched as advice rather than commandments, but it was only traders of the stature of Tatsuma who routinely ignored the triumvirate.

Some trades did create disagreement, and while it was rare, it certainly wasn't unheard of for traders to get on the wrong side of each other and go to war over conflicting positions. Disputes were accepted and debates were encouraged within The House. But with pasts trading the outcomes of skirmishes tended to be immediate and devastating. The House had a deep shared memory of failure, and had learnt to act cooperatively as they came to occupy their central place within all of time.

"Good morning." Said Vance at the London desk, "The present is mixed. The Hang Seng is down three percent, and the NASDAQ is expected to open up half a percent. Copper prices are falling, and crude is strengthening. Ten year bond prices continue to improve as per our actions. Pasts are realigning to The Challenger Trade. The Medici Fabric trade continues to outperform. Today we are moving aggressively on The Napalm Trade. You will find a final briefing in your inbox. Rebalancing orders will be attached for relevant traders, managers, and brokers. Tallulah Dandieu is the lead trader on this past. She will now brief you."

Tallie sat a few desks over, idly scratching her belly. "Good morning." She began.

The Past Trader

27.

The spill was blowing out. She wasn't entirely sure what was happening. But Banthour wasn't moving fast enough and the ancestors of Dow were only getting stronger.

The House pushed out a large capital block. One point four billion, moved into the market at a firesale. It started to budge the past, but it wasn't budging enough.

Tatsuma messaged her: [There's too much wreckage.]

There wasn't enough capital in the right spaces. Lines weren't weaving together.

She tried to make a conscious effort to think about when the war had ended. She thought it had been in June. No, it must have been. Fuck.

She calculated the loss. Four point five billion.

A string of texts came in from Shintaro:

[This is ugly.] [Those 60s 70s antecedents] [They're linking into 76 Persian shares] [Those Iranian enterprises. They didn't used to be state owned.]

[Oh shit.] She replied, [I thought some had survived.]

Tallie smiled.

28.

Tallie arrived at her London house. She had owned this place for almost four years but had never stayed here so it didn't feel at all like home. She walked through to the kitchen where the planes of the summer's rays cut through the afternoon air like golden footpaths.

There was a small box waiting for her on the table. The postmarks were from Lahore.

She opened it cautiously, wondering what trap awaited her. Inside was something thickly covered in tape and bubblewrap. She pried the layers apart and discovered a small ceramic bowl hiding in the center. She turned it over in her hands then placed it carefully on the table in front of her.

She checked the delivery box for a note. There was nothing. She looked closely at the little bowl. She was almost certain that this was a most delicate and meticulous application of Urushi lacquer upon a primitive Jomon style.

29.

Jimmy awoke within the ethereal and presumed that he must have died. Stars were falling out of the sky, drifting on the wind like cosmic feathers. He tried to blink away the sleep and the confusion. A billion orbs of searing light.

He heard yelling in Ukrainian, and had to think for a few moments to piece together what they were saying. "*Zapalnyy! Zapalnyy!! Vohon!*"

Fire? He wondered. Oh fuck.

He was bivouacked under an open sleeping bag, his hand clutching his rifle. He yanked off the makeshift bedding and grabbed up his webbing beside him.

They were in thick woods.

All the men around him were scrambling in a panic to find cover. The lit-up sky was falling on to their heads from all directions in inescapable clustering.

The fuckers had saturated the entire area in an incendiary attack.

The tops of the trees began exploding into flame. But the white lights kept falling - just melting through the canopy.

He tried to crawl into the arch between two broken trees and tuck himself fully underneath a trunk.

There was an incredible sharp pain. A burning little glob, white-hot like magnesium, fell on to his thigh and disappeared through his pants. He desperately tried to swat it out. He watched as it seared through flesh, seared through bone.

He screamed.

Epilogue

PRESS RELEASE: BANTHOUR CHEMICAL CLOSES ACQUISITION OF CGDP

Oak Ridge, Tennessee (5/3/82) - Chemical and industrial process conglomerate, Banthour Chemical, has been successfully chosen to purchase, operate, and upgrade the Chickasaw Gaseous Diffusion Plant (CGDP) in collaboration with the Department of Energy (DoE) and Department of Defence (DoD). Banthour will take responsibility for the enrichment of domestic uranium, the provision of nuclear feedstock, as well as the ongoing maintenance and disposal of the nuclear waste stockpile.

In a public tender, Banthour beat out competitors including Honeywell, Lockheed Martin, and Enron for this multi-decade deal that will ensure Banthour's role in the world's nuclear future. Banthour CEO, Chip Halstead, welcomed the news and emphasized Banthour's market leadership: "Last year's acquisition of Positron Systems provided us the opportunity to expand our business from munition chemicals into radioactive armament, processing, and supply. This huge win for Banthour is definitive proof of our ability to scale and deliver long-lasting value to our shareholders. Banthour is excited to have been recognized as a government partner for delivering the world's oil-free future."

DOE Secretary, Owen Kirby, emphasized the importance of Banthour's role in the nation's energy security: "Ensuring the stability of our nuclear future has been a goal of this administration and we are proud to say that we are delivering on it. We chose Banthour Chemical because they are a reliable partner who deliver world-class service while providing great value for taxpayers."

Details of forecasted revenues, costs, and capital expenditure will be shared during our mid-year earnings report.

Contact:
Suzie Green, Investor Relations
Banthour Chemical International
Chestnut Square, 241 Center Road, Wilmington, Delaware, 19805
Cable Address: BanthourChem
Telex: 11271 & 11238

About the Author

A.M. Donohoo is an Australian who has lived across the globe. He has worked a variety of careers including as a Hollywood magazine editor and as a hedge fund analyst. He interviewed Pamela Anderson on her daybed, and Dua Lipa during a psychic reading. He holds degrees in physics, astronomy & astrophysics, law, and English literature. He has traded many things, including his past for a brighter future.

www.ingramcontent.com/pod-product-compliance
Lightning Source LLC
Chambersburg PA
CBHW030638120726
47904CB00006B/2195